Lock Down Publications and Ca$h
Presents

I0680406

THESE
VICIOUS STREETS
3
Wicked Ambitions

By
Gritty and Raw Crime Novelist
Prince A. Tauhid

First Edition 2024

Printed in the United States of America

This is a work of fiction. Names, characters, places, and incidents either are products of the author's imagination or are used fictitiously. Any similarity to actual events or locales or persons, living or dead, is entirely coincidental.

Lock Down Publications
P.O. Box 944
Stockbridge, GA 30281
www.lockdownpublications.com

Like our page on Facebook: Lock Down Publications
www.facebook.com/lockdownpublications.ldp

Stay Connected with Us!

Text **LOCKDOWN** to 22828 to stay up-to-date with new releases, sneak peaks, contests and more…

Like our page on Facebook:
Lock Down Publications

Join Lock Down Publications/The New Era Reading Group

Visit our website:
www.lockdownpublications.com

Follow us on Instagram:
Lock Down Publications

Email Us: We want to hear from you!

PROLOGUE

Years Earlier

In the beginning, they all were just a bunch of money-hungry, low-life, school dropouts and street thugs, roaming the ghetto and looking to make a quick dollar, no matter how it came. Rather than from a drug sale, a robbery, or some other ill-hearted scheme to get it. They all had ambitions to rise in the hood and finally become somebody. A kingpin hustler even. However wishful their thinking was, there was none to generate from a good nature. It was all evil, and nothing could change that.

There was Kendrick Taylor aka "KT," Jermaine Styles aka "Black Jermaine" or "Dark Skinned Jermaine," Barry Murdoch aka "Murder," Herbert Glover aka "Herb," Jabari, and Garrett Culpepper aka "G-Code." Their territory was in North Philly, in the "BadLands," and the product of choice they sold was crack cocaine, courtesy of Barry and Jabari's cousin named Shepard Murdoch aka "Shep." He was the one to supply them all.

Over time, Shep switched up with his hustle and became a heroin dealer, a world he couldn't afford to invite the teenagers into. He relocated to West Philly and continued to rise in the game, leaving the young bucks the leeway to do as they so pleased on the opposite side of town. They continued on with peddling bundles of coke of their own accord, as they had to make ends meet. Jabari was the one who made the decision to go back to school and sought to become somebody in that regard. He proceeded on to the military upon graduating, then became a cop.

A leader emerged from the six remaining rascals, and he was looking to move the crew in the direction he thought best. This was KT. However, Barry had other plans, also the popularity over the others to have them back him as the leader. The bickering created an internal problem that made for a deadly conclusion.

The very first killing Barry committed was one against his own homeboy when he took out KT. No one knew of this except him and Black Jermaine. He played a part to help set it up, by luring KT to an abandoned house one night, claiming he had the responsible person who had stolen drugs from them tied up there. The theft had occurred two days prior. But once there, Barry appeared from behind KT with his gun trained on the poor boy and shot him down there on the spot. He was able to take over the crew and the supply line from that point. No one dared interfere.

Black Jermaine went along with it because he was a little older, more streetwise, and had a certain level of influence over Barry. But then, Barry began to rack up bodies for his cousin Shep and of his own doing, and gained the nickname "Murder," therefore, forcing Jermaine to fall back to do his own thing but still on "Murder's turf." This couldn't be so without one looking to put the other away. Murder beat Jermaine with getting to the opportunity first. And to prevent from having to resort to killing him over differences of opinions, he set him up to go off to prison, effectively removing Jermaine out of his way so as to make a rise as he never had.

Murder kept Herb close to him, along with Herb's cousin Oskino, G-Code, and a white boy homie of theirs named Douglas James aka "DJ." Through the years, they crossed over from selling coke to heroin. Shep was the main supplier at first, then Jabari began to make magic happen when he met Gustavo Ruiz. The rest as they say, is history.

Those vicious streets of Philly made them all and created the evil ambitions they'd begun to possess. Likewise, it could also be said the same of their own undoing to bring them down and send them away to their graves, or to prison to dwell for the rest of their lives. It's good to have ambitions. However, it's never so when they are wicked. Which side of the streets will they each remain?

PART ONE

Chapter 1

Herb was now in good standing of his own as a dealer. He took up the offer made to him by his Russian counterpart, Vladimir, and put down three hundred thousand on the pill products, the meth, and the Molly they supplied. The business relationship was doing well, and Herb was on his way to being an independent kingpin, a position he'd never held all the years he'd been in the game.

The beauty about the whole operation with the Russians was, Herb found himself to be the only black guy as a distro along the network. And not only that. He'd earned their trust through Vladimir vehemently vouching for him, and they provided an additional three hundred thousand dollars' worth of supply on consignment, to show him how much they trusted his business.

Herb set up his own distro team with a few of his younger cousins and other dudes from around the way whom he knew had a solid hustle about themselves. The pills turned out to be the biggest sellers. They were opioid based and infused with fentanyl, meth, and other powerful substances. Herb had Adderall as well. The college kids loved those. Especially throughout the weekdays. They got into other habitual vices on the weekends. Philly was a big-time college town. And that meant business began to boom for Herb.

Vladimir, Herb's friend and business partner, happened to be tied in with really powerful people, he and his family rather. His uncle (the brother of Vladimir's father) was the infamous Viktor Bout, the international arms dealer and Russian Mafia figurehead. The U.S. government dubbed Viktor as being the "Merchant of Death" at the time when he was listed on the "Most Wanted" list and finally arrested the guy.

Nonetheless, this particular band of Russian mobsters that operated in Philly and the surrounding, concerned themselves with guns, drugs, and the sale of luxury vehicles. Like all other criminal enterprises, they were in high pursuit of money, power, and respect. They had ties with the Chinese and North Korean contraband dealers in America and abroad. As for Herb, he was fortunate to be handed a stroke of "good luck" at the time when he made the acquaintance with Vladimir at the car dealership. The Bout family accepted all that their own, Vladimir, had to say of his business partner. There was still a need for Herb to prove himself to them further at some point soon. Whether that be through a deadly game of Russian Roulette, or some other measure of test they may put him through. Their business was now deeper than the BMW Herb initially bought from Vladimir, and the Mercedes Benz Herb convinced Murder to buy from the dealership himself.

Vladimir wanted to have a business conversation with Herb. The potential of increasing the amount of product issued on consignment existed. But before any of this could take place, Vladimir was issued a special assignment by his family for him to oversee, and to have Herb carry out for them. A Ukrainian competitor turned threat needed to be bumped out the way. He was a problem for the Bout clan and had to go. A black hitter needed to be tapped for the assassination. An ideal cover-up the target would never see coming. One Ivan Ustinov wouldn't know how to prepare for. Once Ivan was out the way, the Bout family had intentions to then take over the line of business Ivan had in operations—sophisticated goods of contraband—rum, vodka, caviar, tobacco products and other commodities smuggled into the country by way of Ukraine and Russia. However, the first bill of order was to whack Ivan, simple and plain.

"Herbie! My friend. How is everything going for you?" Vladimir asked. He spoke broken English, but well enough for others to understand.

"Everything good, Vlad. This might be the best program I've had going on since I've been a dealer. You're the reason for the season behind my success, my guy. And I thank you," Herb responded. The two were in the garage area of the car dealership.

Vladimir offered a smile to Herb's words, accepting the graciousness he had to offer.

"So, you like the way things are going, huh?"

"Hell yeah, I do. I'm more than thankful you felt I was worthy enough to offer the opportunity."

"And so am I," said Vladimir. "That's why I have a bigger opportunity to offer now. Because I believe you're able to get the job done with this one as well." Vladimir propped up against the side of his black Aston Martin with his arms crossed and his legs right over left as he talked with Herb.

"You say there's bigger opportunity? Bigger opportunity like what?" Herb's interest was now perked up.

Vladimir took a pause to think of how to properly phrase what he wanted to say. He had it. All he needed to do was just say it.

"I want you to remove someone who's blocking the path of progress for me and my people," he declared.

Herb jarred his head at the blunt request Vladimir made.

"You want me to remove someone who's blocking the path of progress for you and your people?" he retorted. Herb put back to Vladimir the same question, word for word, so he'd have the chance to hear how it sounded.

"That's exactly what I need. And once this is to take place, the plan is to increase the amount of supply tremendously that you're moving."

"This must be a really important motherfucker . . . for you to come to me and not contract any of your Russian counterparts," Herb stated.

"My friend. The act of murder doesn't care who commits it, so long as it gets done," Vladimir countered with a touch of rhetoric of his own. "A hitter not from Russian descent, is the perfect cover for this particular mission, Herbie. He'd never detect a thing."

Truth be, Herb wasn't a hitter like that. Not as his friend Murder was. Herb's blood ran warm, while Murder's was cold as Vladimir's motherland of Russia in the winter season. Indeed, Herb had killed before. And two people weren't physically here any longer as proof of those slayings. However, the fact of the matter remained, dude was no killer. There was Murder and Traino who had his back for that purpose. But now, he was being relied upon to do this type of work independently, and Vladimir wasn't in the business to take no for an answer. Not at that point moving forward. This particular mission was part of the main reason why Vladimir so readily welcomed Herb in on the narcotic business to begin with, to eventually get to the point of the hit being ordered, and Herb, the one asked to do it.

Vladimir continued. "Bigger opportunity than you may have ever imagined in this business, Herbie. I can't give the details until I know, yes . . . you'd do it. And I can't accept no for an answer either. We've come too far for that. And you know too much. If you agree to take care of this, it's all good. If you don't agree to, it's all bad. And we Russian thugs don't like bad, Herbie," Vladimir muttered, now standing tall at six foot seven, arms still crossed, and eyeing down Herb with a mean-mug and those penetrating dark pupils in his eyes. His half-inch thick, reddish beard was full in size and sharply lined.

"Well, can I at least have someone tag along with me as my help to take care of this for you?" Herb asked.

"That's not a problem, Herbie. I trust you'll get the job done. So, do we have an agreement here, my friend?" Vladimir asked, then extended his hand to shake Herb's, if he was to agree.

With a bit of reluctance initially, Herb finally agreed. "Yeah, man. We have a deal. I'll do it," he said.

The two shook hands. Vladimir then retrieved a file folder from his car and passed it over to Herb. It was the profile on Ivan Ustinov. They then began to exit the garage.

Vladimir pulled out his cell phone and made a call. The person on the opposite end answered.

"It's done," Vladimir said. "I had my friend to agree. He's gonna do it

Chapter 2

A worker of Felipe Valdez aka "Highway," by the name of Ralphie Arroyo, was busted on a raid at his house. In his possession he had an AR-15, a Glock pistol, a bulletproof vest, and two kilos of heroin from the recent batch Felipe received from Gustavo following the trip. Ralphie already had two prior drug and firearm possession convictions and had served time. He now faced an enhanced federal sentence on the new charges and had more trouble to deal with than he ever knew. The feds had a proposition they wanted to offer, being that they had Ralphie pinned to the ground with no way out.

The head U.S. Attorney in Philadelphia—John Fletcher—passed over Ralphie's case to AUSA Gregory Conner and his female colleague, Felicia Alvarez, to handle things. Fletcher, wanted them to squeeze Ralphie for all they could in the hopes of positioning themselves to secure more arrests and convictions of other bad boys within the enterprise. If Ralphie would talk.

Greg and Felicia were familiar with each other. They maintained an ongoing sexual relationship. This had been so for a year now. The two did a really good job concealing the affair from their supervisor, colleagues, and others in society. However, things were subject to change. In the world of love and war in the workplace, one never knows.

Greg and Felicia began to drill Ralphie in the interrogation room.

"Oh, boy! You're in a lot of trouble here, Ralphie. If only you knew," Greg said, as he flipped through the pages of Ralphie's rap sheet. He'd racked up one hell of a criminal record since beginning a career at age seventeen.

"I'm in a lot of trouble, huh? I'm built for this! I wouldn't be a part of the life if I wasn't. So, fuck you!" Ralphie responded insultingly.

"Oh, yeah. You really are in some deep shit. And I don't plan to respond to your disrespect. But listen to this. What about your family? Your poor mother, who's gonna lose that nice home of hers you paid for with your drug money? What about that lovely daughter of yours, who's gonna be kicked out of college and lose her opportunity to do something with all that smartness she has, due to your ill-gained money funding her education? And probably the most hurtful of them all, what about your two little ones, that's gonna be taken from you and your girlfriend, and placed in foster care, while you and the girlfriend are being hauled off to prison soon, not to ever return? What about all that? And you say, 'Fuck me?' No, buddy! You're the one who's gonna fuck yourself!" Greg replied.

"Damn, AUSA Conner," Ralphie uttered upon taking a look at the name tag of the prosecutor. "You're that heartless? What does my family have to do with me? My actions were not their actions. I was the one who got caught up. Not them. Why you have to include innocent people?"

"We're the ones asking questions here, Arroyo, not you," Felicia chimed in to say.

"Oh my, mami! I didn't mean to light your fuse, my bad," said Ralphie.

"We're not here to play any games with you, Arroyo! Now you're going to give us what we want. Or your family is going to suffer along with you, behind all the wrong you've done. And to remind you once more, your girlfriend will be going to prison right along with you. So don't bullshit with us! We're not gonna tolerate it!" Felicia spat in an aggressive tone while up in Ralphie's face.

Ralphie got quiet and thought over a few things to himself to potentially say so as to avert the government from going after his family as they presented signs of doing. Especially his kids. The four and seven-year-old specifically. He didn't move nor utter a word. He was intent on waiting to hear what more they had to say, so he'd know what all they know.

The prosecutors continued.

"Look, here's what we know, Ralph, ok?" said Greg.

"And if you bullshit us from this point onward, I promise you, we'll have a judge immediately signing an order to have your girlfriend arrested, your mother evicted, your two little kids taken, and your teenage daughter expelled! Now try us if you like! And see what the results will be!" Felicia threatened.

Ralphie looked from Felicia to Greg, then back again. A strong sense of defeat overtook him. He thought over how the end of his run came about in dealing drugs for Felipe Valdez. He then spoke.

"You mentioned knowing a thing or two," he let out, looking specifically at Greg. "I'd like to know what you know. And hopefully, we may be able to agree on a few things. Could you agree to that?" he asked, looking directly at Felicia for an answer.

Being that a threat to his mother and kids' lifestyles were in jeopardy, he felt Felicia would be the one to have more sympathy than Greg. He couldn't have been more wrong than he was in thinking that way.

Felicia slammed an ink pen and a "proffered" document onto the table, then dictated their terms.

"You see, Arroyo, we don't want you. You're a worthless piece of shit to what we're aiming to bring down. Things did get easier when we nailed you with your drugs and the guns you had with the serial numbers filed off. But nonetheless, we really don't want you. We want your boss, Felipe Valdez. What can you provide us about him?" Felicia asked bluntly.

"I might know a thing or two about him. But if I talk, me and my family are off the table as food for the prosecution, right?" Ralphie wanted to know.

"Depending on the quality of your information. Now get to talking!" spat Felicia as she was already up in his face yet again.

***

Major and Highway were back in business again. As promised by Gustavo, the supply was doubled. They now owed two times the money than they normally would. No excuses or shortages would be accepted. Gustavo loved his money. And didn't mind having people killed behind it.

Major was sure to supply Murder with all he was due. Normally, Murder took on twenty-five kilos at a time. But now, he was provided fifty, due to the increase on Major by Gustavo. Murder had to work overtime now, being that Herb moved on to a different product, and he was down a worker or two. He knew dudes around the hood he could lay additional bricks upon and trust they'd pay when the time was at hand. Things would work out. There was no need to fret.

Major invited Murder over to his place for a business discussion. They hadn't seen one another in weeks.

"Barry, listen. I know you weren't notified beforehand about the increase in product I supplied you with. But from here on out, that's how it's got to be. You now have to take double each time."

"What the hell you mean by that? I have to take double each time? I'm having complications moving all the shit I got already! Not to mention, I gotta work extra hard to win back my customers who moved on when I ain't have no product," stated Murder.

"My supplier—"

Murder cut his sentence off midway. "You mean Gustavo, don't you? Gustavo Ruiz," he said, making the fact known that he now knew the name of the Colombian drug trafficker.

Major gave him an odd look. "Yeah . . . Gustavo. That's who I was referring to."

"I just want you to know . . . that I know. I've been informed of it all. Every detail. And we're gonna keep that strictly between you and me, my guy. Alright?"

Major jarred his head and furrowed his eyebrows at Murder's words. He was forced to stop in his tracks as they paced on the lawn in the backyard. The thought then dawned upon him. The very person who turned him on to Gustavo Ruiz, was the brother of the man he now talked with. Therefore, it was needed to at least acknowledge he understood.

"I can agree to that," Major declared.

"Good. Now continue with what you were saying."

"I will. Thank you. Now as I *was* saying, before you rudely interrupted," Major felt the need to regain authority over the conversation, "Gustavo doubled the supply. He shut down the California operation for the time being. And now, the New York and Philly operations must carry the load. Then have his money ready in the same thirty-day time period as the normal amount of product sold in that cycle. This is so to take up the slack for the West Coast stoppage," Major explained.

"Once I get everything up and going smoothly like I had before, that shouldn't be a problem. The product is good quality anyway. It'll sell itself. Always does," Murder said.

"Right. You got it together. You know what to do. And being that you've already paid half the money up front, you're halfway there."

"Ain't no doubt about that. I'm a hustla,' Major. That's what I do. I get rid of products. That's my occupation, to move dope. Now, all I need you to do is be sure to keep in mind everything we agreed to, nigga. That's all you need to do."

"And all I need you to do is, be sure you got that bread ready for me by the time these thirty days are up," Major quickly fired back. "And although you now know as much as I do, don't forget, Barry, *I'm* the one in charge here, young nigga, stay in your lane. And I'll keep in mine. We can't lose doing it this way."

The street shit Major had in him came out in that instance. He knew it was necessary to put Murder back in his place and not allow him any leeway to think for once that he was the one calling the shots, and not Major himself. And had he not, a problem was possibly brewing.

Murder produced a smirk at Major behind his words. Inside, Murder actually applauded him, for finally showing more aggression than he usually would. Murder spoke out more. "It's about damn time, nigga! I need to see more of that street shit come out you from here on out. I might begin to like you more then. Ol' square-ass nigga!" Murder said, then chuckled like crazy as he walked away. "And tell that nigga C-Ro I say what up. We making this paper again," he lastly said before turning the corner of the house and now out of sight.

Murder then made his way home, back to the penthouse, to think over ways to get creative and incorporate into his hustling schemes. The timing of it all worked out to Murder's advantage. He was beginning to get impatient with the process and had even contemplated a move to go against Major. Nonetheless, in the nick of time, Jabari intervened and provided the little brother the rundown of it all, sparing Major any future problems he had no knowledge of, that was about to be dealt against him.

Jabari knew how thin Murder's tolerance level was. He figured correctly that Murder was up to something, with all the questions he had. And that became the main reason why Jabari took the initiative to inform Murder on what the delay was all about. To prevent Major any harm from coming his way. His predictions were accurate, and things flowed smoothly once the story was told.

The team that was silently led by Jabari, was again moving aggressively towards the top. All the bumps in the road along with the bullshit, was now cleared out the way.

Chapter 3

Quana and Tatiana were together on this day. They were en route to Tati's dad's spot to check in on their twin parents and to say hello. While riding in Quana's car, the two young females held a conversation. Quana was busy trying to figure out a few things from the words Tati allowed to exit her mouth. And this particular in-depth talk with the one person she was suspicious about, could possibly enlighten her on what it was she sought to know. To her, it was worth a shot.

"Tati, look. You know that shit we did together gotta stay strictly between us, right? Because if not, it could cause all types of problems for not only us, but this family as a whole. And you already know, family is something I strongly believe in," Quana stated, as she steered the car and maintained a stern look at Tati, displaying how serious she was.

"I'm already knowing, Quana. That goes without saying. But I really feel like you getting at something else," Tati responded, urging Quana to go ahead and spit out what she really wanted to say.

"That's because I am. Your feeling is on point." Quana's comeback had a somewhat harsh tone to it. She definitely had something on her breasts she wanted to get off. Something she'd been holding onto.

"Well, what is it? You know you can be straight up with me about whatever," stated Tati. Her heart began to pound ferociously. She had a fear Quana may have found out something about her sneaking behind her back and fucking her boyfriend on the low.

"How do I know you told me the truth about that chick we knocked off? That bro paid you to do it? Because something is not adding up for me." Quana put two powerful questions on Tati.

"Because, Quana, that's the truth. I have no reason to lie. But why you say that though?"

"I do because I know my brother. If he was the one behind something like that, he would've tapped me to do it. Or asked do I know some other trustworthy female who I could have do it with me. Besides, at the time, you hadn't even been back home that long for him to immediately come to you and ask you to do something like that. There wasn't enough time in between for him to have had the chance to check you out to know he could trust you enough for that. Not that type of work. That's why I say that," Quana stated in a matter-of-fact tone of voice.

"Well . . . truth is —"

Quana cut her words short. "And how do I even know that female was somebody my brother wanted gone? Not to mention, a pregnant female! With me knowing how bad my brother wants a kid. Something not adding up. For all I know, that could've been a female who was pregnant by the boyfriend you claimed to have broken up with around the time. If not, convince me otherwise then," Quana stated. She spoke in her signature tone of fierceness. There was a slight snarl to it. The thought of Tati or Heeme not answering their phones that night passed through her mind. Repeated calls were made. There was no reason why neither of the two couldn't at least have replied to the text message and voicemails sent. Both means of contact will always come through, the very moment their cell phones were powered back on. The thought added further insult to injury.

"Quana!" Tati exclaimed. "Cuz! What the fuck you on!" Tati had a hard look at Quana. She held her mouth wide while doing so. She couldn't believe the accusation her cousin was casting upon her. "You accusing me of something, Quana? Because I didn't even know that girl. Neither did Neko. And I couldn't give two fucks about who he deal with or gets pregnant. Me and him are done! He can have whoever. And I can move on with whoever I'mma do so with when I get ready to." The thought of Heeme passed through her mind. "And that's all there is to it. So now what?" she let out, sitting upright in the passenger seat and returning the same look of seriousness Quana had.

The collar of Tati's shirt was lying flat, exposing a large hickey on the left side of her neck. She tried her hardest to hide it, so as to keep the questions away. It was too late. Her and Heeme's secret activities was now one step further in the open. Quana spotted it but kept it to herself.

"Okay. Pipe down, you lil' half-bred, Puerto Rican bitch! I ain't accusing you of nothing. I was just saying. That's all," Quana fired back. She knew Tati well enough to know that her cousin wasn't going to let go so easily, a shot like that at her character without at least firing back. They were too much alike. However, Quana was setting her up for something more. She knew Tati would go to the ends of the earth to prove her innocence of something. That's exactly what happened.

"Quana, that shit didn't come off too well! And I don't appreciate it either! You coming for me like that. Then talking about, 'you just saying!' What the fuck are you saying? 'Cause we can call Barry right now to get that shit straight there!" Tati spat, totally forgetting all about the fact that Murder told her not to mention anything to anyone. Not to mention the fact he paid her to do the hit all by herself. She was beginning to fuck up bad. And had no clue that she was.

"You said exactly what I thought you would. Let's do just that. Let's call bro," Quana stated as she was now parking the car in front of Dollar Bill's apartment. They had arrived.

"Yeah! Let's do just that, Quana! Because I ain't got shit to hide," Tati replied. She now had her phone palmed in her hand going through the contacts.

"The number has changed since you last talked to him. I'll call him up on my phone here," Quana said to her, retrieving her phone from the bag she carried.

Tati came to a stop in going through her contact list at the point. Quana was looking on while she done so. There was something that caught Quana's eye on the large screen of Tati's phone. She didn't know exactly why, but her cousin always had a bad habit of buying phones with oversize screens. The one she now had was the latest model Galaxy Note, the only device at the time with a seven-inch screen.

The particular thing to gain Quana's attention was the name of a contact. It read, "The Dream," a word that rhymed with "Raheem," Heeme's government. Upon taking notice, it brought to mind a statement Tati had made when she first got back home to Philly and Quana mentioned that her and Heeme were still together. Tati had asked, *"So cuz, who you got in your life now? You always keep some type of dope ass thug nigga somewhere in the mix. I'm hoping to find me one now. Neko didn't live up to the hype."*

Quana responded, *"Ain't nobody new, cuz. It's still me and my man, Raheem. Nothing changed. It only got better."*

"Well, okay then! You and Raheem, still living the dream, ain't y'all," Tati had said.

Her words became situated in Quana's mind, in the exact way that she worded it, "The Dream." It was those two words that stood out most of all. And now there they were, as a contact in the phone of the person who uniquely expressed them the time prior to the day.

Quana jarred her head and squinted her eyes at Tati from anger. She badly wanted smoke today but held back from doing so. Her control over impulse was maintained. A rare thing for Quana.

There was a new game she now had to play. It was called, *"catch a no-good bitch sneaking around with her man!"*

Quana had Murder's number pulled from contacts and now on the screen of the phone. All she had to do was hit send. For some reason, she paused.

"You know what," she let out, then began deleting the contact from processing a call. "I was testing you to see how well you would hold up. You're fucking up, Tati, and bad too! Bro told you not to mention shit to nobody. Nobody means me too! So let that shit marinate. And do better, bitch! You could fuck up and get us in a lot of trouble if you don't. A'ight, bitch? Now, get-your-shit-together. And be sure to keep it that way. Don't let me have to tell you twice," Quana spat in a serious tone of voice.

Tati looked on at her in a nervous yet shocked type of way. Both her mouth and eyes were wide. A level of fear overtook her once more.

"I got you on that, cuz. I understand," Tati said.

But in all honesty, did she really?

Quana had an entirely different puzzle to piece together at this point. One she would most likely have no problem constructing. Eventually.

Quana locked eyes with Tati and fixed her face into a scary mask. She had something else to say to Tati. Something she absolutely wanted her to know she was dead-ass serious about.

"Tatiana. Cuz, listen. I want you to hear me out and hear me well on this, ok? The only time you may ever have to worry about me coming for you, will be if I was to find out anything about you sneaking and creeping on the low with my man—Raheem the 'Dream' Jones—just like the —" Quana cut her own words short. "You know what," she began once more. "It'll be best if I keep that to myself. Come on. Let's go in, and see how our twin parents are doing, shall we?" she said.

Quana was able to get the exact reaction she'd hoped for. At the mention of the words, "The Dream," Tatiana unconsciously allowed her head to look downward at her phone. This was a definite sign of guilt in Quana's understanding. She had it in mind to bring up the topic at a later time and date. At the point of which she would be ready to deal with it fully.

The two girls entered Dollar Bill's apartment. Tati had a key. They couldn't believe their eyes. The sight of their parents was atrocious to look upon. The appearance and condition they were in. Karen and Dollar Bill were high as shit! They both were sweaty and reeked of a foul odor. They had too much going on. This was the result of being up several days without a shower, and on a mission to get high.

"Momma! Uncle Kev!" Quana yelled out.

"Yo, look at you two! Tati chimed in to say. "We not about to let y'all two go on like this. Y'all about to get y'all shit together."

"Momma, I'm about to take your behind to my place, so you can shower and get some rest. You and Uncle Kev can get back to it some other time," Quana said to her mother.

"Baby, wait. Wait, baby. Please. Hold on," Karen pleaded with her daughter as Quana held her tightly by the arm and was dragging her towards the bedroom to get her belongings. "Baby, please don't say anything to your brother, ok? Please, Quana! He don't know nothing about me getting high, does he? Barry wouldn't understand. This is what I wanna do."

"I'm not gonna say anything to Barry, Momma. I just want you to shower and get a little rest, before you and Uncle Kev OD over here on us. That's all," Quana stated to her mother.

Karen was terrified of her son.

"Okay, baby, no problem. You know I love spending time with your Uncle Kev there."

"Yeah, Daddy. You're about to do the same thing too. Get a shower and some sleep! And I'm not gonna take any of your bullshit about it either, Dollar Bill," Tati said to her father as she began to escort him to the bathroom to shower.

"I'll talk with you later, cuz. Let me get Momma on over to my place and help her situate herself," Quana said to Tati.

She now had all her mother's belongings packed and ready to roll. Everything but her drug paraphernalia. That was left behind. More than likely, it'd be there when she returned.

Quana speed-walked with her mother to the car. "You better hurry up and get your ass in before somebody spots us and call Barry," Quana warned.

"I damn sure better, huh," Karen responded, then quickly hopped in the car so they could be on their way.

No sooner than the daughter and mother pulled away, Tatiana went into the back room of the apartment, unlocked her phone, and hit the contact icon that read, "The Dream." Heeme answered on the opposite end. He was eager to talk with Tati once more.

***

Thirty Minutes Later . . .

Heeme arrived at Dollar Bill's apartment to pick up Tati. Before leaving to go with dude, she was sure to give her dad damn near an overdose of sleeping pills to put his ass out. The two then hit the Roosevelt Boulevard en route to the Howard-Johnson Hotel in northeast Philly.

Tati had so much she wanted to relate to him, and much more she wanted to do. She yearned like crazy for the dick since he first had the opportunity to put it on her. Tati also had money to give him, as he had her moving the heroin product that was stolen from Murder and Herb. He was now down to five kilos. They were stashed at his spot down in South Philly.

Tati and Heeme made it to the hotel and were inside the suite. They only had enough time to get out of their clothes and begin foreplay before Heeme's phone vibrated. He had a call. It slipped his mind to turn it off yet again. Dude was asking for trouble. He took a look at the screen.

"Fuck!" he let out.

The call was from Quana. She was checking in on him. Tati came up from sucking his dick. "What, Heeme?" she asked.

"Quana calling," he revealed. His phone began to vibrate yet again.

Tati smirked behind his words. She locked eyes with him and then shrugged her shoulders. "So! Let that bitch keep calling. Cum thicka' than blood the way I see it! That bitch gotta wait her turn now, Heeme. It's on me today," she stated, then went back down on him to suck him off more.

Heeme looked on at her and laughed, then continued to enjoy the sensation he experienced behind Tati pulling on his dick with those sexy pink lips of hers. Heeme then lay on the bed and propped up on a pillow. Tati hopped atop now and proceeded to work him well. He tilted his head to the back and stretched out further, totally ignoring the fact that he had a psychopath for a girlfriend, who was about to go berserk if his ass didn't make it his business to answer that damn phone immediately. He still refused, taking pleasure in the outstanding blow job the biracial beauty was giving him.

Next, the text messages and voicemails began to flood his phone. Shortly thereafter, a shift occurred, from Heeme's phone to Tati's. The two was so caught up in the moment and into one another, even she didn't think to turn off her phone. Quana's rage was being unleashed a little at a time. She didn't stop in her attempts to contact the two. If only they had any idea what the fuck they were causing, they probably would've left it alone well ahead of time.

***

Quana rushed from her house, hopped in her car, and began the drive to Heeme's apartment.

When she arrived, she didn't see his car anywhere in sight. She'd let herself in with the duplicate key Heeme knew nothing about. The slick bitch made a copy from the original. Quana went straight to the bedroom closet where she knew he still had the money and those last kilos of heroin stashed. Dude had everything neatly situated in Jordan shoe boxes. Those were his favorite brand of sneakers. The hundred grand the two counted out that night was still there. Heeme's plan was to sell out of everything before doing a re-up with the money. Possibly on a different product. Coke maybe. However, that particular plan was about to become a pipe dream. All because he couldn't maintain control of his dick and sexual desires.

Quana grabbed the money and the product, dumped it into a pillowcase, left out Heeme's place, and drove back home.

She had a thought. *That bitch-ass nigga wanna play games with me*! *I got something for his ass*!

Once inside her house, she went to her bedroom, locked the door behind herself to keep from being disturbed by her mom who was in the back room, and got busy taking pictures of the heroin and money to send to Heeme as proof to show she wasn't playing any games. Quana wasn't about the bullshit any longer. The nigga Heeme had really fucked up, whether he knew it had gotten that serious or not. Heeme now had hell to pay for his pleasure.

Quana put away the money and drugs in her closet, on the same shelf as the new sets of clothing she'd recently bought her mother, along with the clean clothing Karen had on hand.

Quana then exited her bedroom and made her way back out the door. The plan was to now head over to West Philly to Tatiana's house. Karen was laid out on the couch, tossing back and forth trying like hell to sleep. She had eaten and taken a shower. Her body was in the process of shutting down to relax.

Before going over to West Philly, Quana made a stop back by her uncle Dollar Bill's apartment. This was the last place she knew Tati to be. In the place where she left her. Her instincts proved correct. Tati was not there. She was gone. Dollar Bill was barely able to get up to answer the door. Nonetheless, he managed to do so.

I knew that slimy low-down half-breed bitch was up to no good! Quana thought upon discovering Tati wasn't there any longer. *I seen it with my own two eyes in that bitch's phone! The first time could've been a coincidence. But twice now without being able to locate either of the two and not answering their phones? That's too much. It's deliberate. Ain't nothing else to leave for questioning! Them bitches fuckin' around behind my motherfucking back! And I'm about to check that shit!* Quana vented in her own mind.

She had her pistol with her now inside her tote bag. It was a Glock-17, a weapon for protection her brother bought her. Quana had vehement intentions at this point. The very moment she was to catch her boyfriend and cousin together, she was going to fire their asses up then and there on the spot.

The pictures she'd taken of the heroin and the money hadn't been sent as of yet, nor the threatening text messages and voicemails she'd saved for Tatiana. She wanted to wait until a specific time to do so because she knew once she did, Heeme would come running her way, and she was trying to catch him up.

Quana left Dollar Bill's spot and was now on the way to Tati's house. When she arrived, she saw that her car was there, but the lights were off inside the house. She got out of her car and knocked on the door. She tried numerous times to give Tati the benefit of the doubt. There was no one to answer. No Tatiana. No anyone. It was on and popping now. There wasn't anything left to figure out. It was a wrap. Whether her ill intentions was to lead to one count of murder or two, Quana's mind was made up. She wanted to take action for being played in the way she had, like a fool. And then laughed at behind her back. She began to cry.

I'mma kill both them bitches! *I put that on my unborn baby's soul*! She thought. The venting became more intense.

Quana was three weeks pregnant with Heeme's seed.

Chapter 4

Earlier in the day...

Murder was up at the crack of dawn and on the move about town making drop-offs and moving the product he now had. He and Herb usually would do this at the same time, but that was no more. Also, Murder had the duty to situate damn near one hundred kilos of heroin to the many stash spots designated for the purpose. He had new storage units to hide product in, and the home he owned in Lower Marion. Quana's house was also a location he utilized to put his material. This was the largest amount of narcotics Murder had ever held at one time.

He had a thought.

I bet once that nigga Herb got word I got raw shit back out on the streets again he's gonna try to hop right back on my jock again. And this nigga talkin' about the dope game beginning to play out! Shhh! That nigga done lost his goddamn mind! I'mma show him that the business of dope is gonna always be alive and poppin'! This shit will never die!

The car Murder had the kilos in was a new model Nissan Altima that was to go to Quana's house later in the day. He had it parked in a pay garage that was located not too far away from where he was in his penthouse suite downtown. His intention was to rest up for a while to about midday then head on over to Quana's. He was tired from all the moving around he'd done throughout the wee hours of the A.M. The time was 8:30 A.M.

***

Eleven Hours Later . . .

Murder finally awakened from the so-called 'nap' he had taken. He'd overslept. The sleeping pills had put him out.

His phone vibrated. It was laying on the floor next to the bed. He rolled over and grabbed it. The number on the screen was from Maryland.

Mom and Randle, he thought.

He hadn't heard from the two in weeks.

Let me see what they talking about, he further thought.

"Hello!" Murder answered.

"Barry. What's good, son? How you been?" Karen's boyfriend said.

"Hey. What's up, Randle? I'm good, man. What about you?"

"I'm taking things easy myself. Or at least I'm trying to," Randle expressed.

Murder caught on to the distress in his voice.

"Oh, man. What now, Randle?" Murder asked, basically urging him to go on and spit it out.

"Is now a good time for you?"

"Randle! Spit it out, dude! What has Mom done now? I know she's done something. This the only time I get to speak to you first," Murder uttered.

"Your mom, Barry. She was supposed to have returned home after one weekend there. That was almost three weeks ago. And —"

"Wait-wait-wait! Hold up. What you mean, she was supposed to have returned home after a weekend here!" Murder retorted. "I don't know nothing about Mom being back in Philly. And why you just now calling me to say something about it? You know better than that, Randle. Y'all bugging!" he further vented.

"I know, Barry. True indeed, I should've said something sooner. I apologize about that. But your mother begged me not to say anything to you. She wanted to visit home to see Quana and Kevin."

"Randle! Again, why the fuck are you just now telling me this, dude!" Murder spat as he began to get up out of bed to get dressed.

"She begged me not to say anything to you, Barry. And you know I don't want Karen pissed at me," Randle continued trying to explain.

Murder began to get so heated with his mom, that he completely bypassed the bathroom to brush his teeth and wash his face en route out the front door.

"I understand, man. It's all good, but your ass needs to start back wearing the boxers in the house down there and not Karen. And when I bought that house for you two, didn't I tell you that you were the man of the house?"

"Yeah. You did," Randle replied.

"Well then, act like it, nigga!" Murder let out to the white boyfriend his mom loved so dearly. "And stop letting Karen run over you. Put your foot down and let her know you mean business."

"You're right, Barry. I will."

"And by the way, when was the last time you had a chance to talk to her?"

"About two weeks ago," Randle answered.

"About two weeks ago! Nigga!"

"Yep. haven't since. Her phone goes straight to voicemail now. And I tried to call Shaquana at her number. Same results."

Truth be, Karen was too busy getting high with Dollar Bill. Neither of the two wanted to be bothered. By no one. Karen simply turned her phone off and expected her boyfriend to follow her orders to the letter.

Randle held out for as long as he could. He then gave in, as there were two things he feared most by Karen being away that long. One, she'd possibly relapsed and started back shooting dope, or two, she was out with another man and cheating on him. He had no clue what the fuck Karen was busy being up to.

"I'm on my way out the door now, Randle, to go find her ass. I'll hit you back when I do. A'ight?" Murder said to him.

"Okay, Barry. Be easy on her, man. And don't be mad at me."

"Oh, I'mma be easy on her alright! Right up-side her goddamn head all the way back down to Maryland!" Murder lastly spat then killed the call.

Nearly twenty minutes later, Murder was pulling up to Dollar Bill's apartment. He got out of the Escalade and banged like a madman on the door.

"I'm coming, I'm coming! Wait a minute, damn it!" Dollar Bill let out, as he staggered from the bedroom, through the short hallway and to the living room, having to brace himself along the walls for balance, to keep from falling to the floor.

He opened the door. Murder bust in.

"Where the fuck she at, Dollar Bill? Huh! Where Moms at?" Murder spat. He then jacked Dollar Bill up by the dingy button-down church shirt he had on.

Dollar Bill was still high as a scud-missile.

Murder took a menacing look around the area of the living room. Evidence showed two people were indeed there at one point and had had themselves one hell of a good time. There were beer bottles, ash trays, and other essentials that addicts keep on hand when doing their thing. The most disturbing for Murder, was the paraphernalia kits he spotted on the floor.

"Where the fuck she at, Dollar Bill? I see she fuckin' with that dope again too, ain't she?" Murder hissed through gritted teeth.

"She gone, man. She left with your sister to go rest up for a while so she can head on back home. Baby sis just wanted to have a little fun, nephew. That's all," Dollar Bill said, trying to help his nephew properly understand exactly who his mom was and all she loved to do. Even if that meant every so often.

A tear skipped down Murder's face as he continued to mean-mug Dollar Bill and grip tightly on his shirt. Slowly, he unclenched his fist from Dollar Bill's shirt and eased back. He then walked out the apartment and got back into his truck.

If anything, being the dope dealer he was and had been for many years, Murder knew what the raw reality of life was like in the game. And it made no difference what side of the equation one was on, whether user or dealer. The fact of the matter always stood true, once a hustler always a hustler, and once a junkie always that as well. All Murder wanted was to hear it for himself, from his mother. Straight from her mouth. And then, maybe he would live better knowing this was what she wanted to do with her life, get high at times and be sober at times. He simply wanted Karen to look him in the face and tell him what the deal was.

Murder began the drive to Quana's house located in the Kensington neighborhood. He had so much to think over along the way.

Chapter 5

Quana was now parked at a distance down the block from Tati's house on the opposite side of the street. The night was now setting in, and her black BMW wasn't so easy to spot, if Heeme and Tati were on the lookout once he dropped her back off. Quana was sure the scenario would play out exactly in this way. How so? Because of those photos of the kilos and the money. She'd sent them to Heeme with a threatening text message, and knew without a doubt, his ass would come running full speed ahead at any moment's notice. And if he had Tati away with him, he would have to drop her off at home first before he made his way to her place to argue about what she'd done. A smart move played well on Quana's behalf.

Both Tati and Heeme knew he couldn't take her back to her dad's apartment, since that was the last location where Quana had left Tati. And she was to return to pick Tati back up once she situated her mom at her place and made a run to the grocery store to get Karen a few of her favorite snacks and feminine products of her choice. Quana knew her mother's preference. Also, Quana did have her gun on her, locked and loaded, ready to blast.

Not too much longer, just like Quana accurately speculated, up pulled Heeme's light gray Dodge Charger in front of Tati's place. The interior light came on, indicating the door to the passenger side had opened. Tati was trying to hurry and get out. Heeme pulled her back to him for a kiss to end their occasion for that day. There was no telling when they would have the opportunity to do the same again. Quana was looking on the whole time. She saw it all, with her own two eyes. She was about to go bananas.

"Motherfucka' you!" she yelled out while in a rush to get from the car.

Quana then began running in the direction of the two.

Boom-Boom-Boom-Boom-Boom-Boom-Boom!

Multiple rounds were fired. Her intent was to kill. Nothing else.

Heeme's car was hit. Bullets whizzed past Tati, narrowly missing as she raised up from the vehicle. Heeme then stomped the gas pedal of the muscle car, fishtailing from the curb. Tati took off running wide open down the street, going the opposite direction.

As Heeme corrected and passed Quana, she fired more shots.

Boom-Boom-Boom-Boom!

He was hit in the left shoulder as he slumped low trying to avoid the possibility. He made it past and was now in the clear. Heeme knew who it was. He'd heard the voice and seen her face. The boy continued in his drive, now on the way to go get medical help.

Quana got back into her car. It was still running. She then sped off on her way home to lay low and call her brother to let him know what was up.

***

Meanwhile ...

Murder finally made it to Quana's house from Dollar Bill's spot. He had a key and let himself in.

"Where you at, Ma? I know your ass in here!" he barked upon entering and heading straight to the back bedroom.

Murder laid his eyes upon his mother. He'd awakened her from sleeping.

"What the fuck, Ma! Huh! You just had to go back to that world, didn't you! It was impossible for you to stay away, wasn't it?" he further vented. He then snatched the cover off of her.

"Barry! Barry! It's okay, son. Momma good. I just wanted to play for a little while. That's all. I promise I can handle it. I'm not gonna get outta control," Karen responded, not realizing she'd already broken the trust her son and boyfriend had for her.

"Yeah! You can handle that shit all right. If that was the case, why the fuck Randle had to call me to let me know your ass been here in Philly for the past three weeks and going, and he ain't heard shit from you! Huh! Tell me that, Miss, I can handle it!" he scolded further. "Get up! I'm about to have Quana take your ass home right now!"

Murder then roughly grabbed his mother by the arm and was in the mindset to escort her to the closet where her clothes were located when his cell phone vibrated. It was his sister.

"Yeah! What up, Quana! And your black ass got a lot of explaining to do —"

"Bro, I need your help!" Quana cut him off to say. "Some shit just popped off, yo!"

"Wait a minute. Calm down. What the fuck!"

"Some shit popped off, bro! It was that bitch-ass nigga Heeme and a jawn! Our slimy-ass cousin, Tatiana!" she let him know. Quana continued to drive in the direction of her house from out West Philly.

"Heeme and Tatiana! What?" he responded in shock.

"Yeah, bro! Those two. And I made it my business to get at 'em both! Like, for real, for real too!"

"Yo, where the fuck you at?" Murder asked.

"I'm on my way from out West Philly. Meet me at my spot."

"How about, I'm already at your spot? Me and Moms! How you explain that shit?"

"I'll be there in a minute, Barry. And Mom not the issue anymore," Quana declared.

"Look. Just hurry and get your ass here right now! That's all you do!" Murder spat and then ended the call.

He then got back to dealing with his mother. He grabbed her by the arm yet again and began to drag her to the closet where he assumed her clothes were.

"Wait up, Barry. Okay? Quana got all my belongings and other stuff in the closet in her room," Karen made him aware.

"Okay, well let's go get your shit out of there and be ready for her to take your ass back to Maryland."

Murder then pulled her by the arm all the way to the closet in Quana's bedroom. Once there, he noticed her bag and other material he knew belonged to her situated on the top shelf. He assumed everything was Karen's and began yanking it from its place in an angry manner.

Murder noticed one of the black nylon bags was a little heavier than it should have been. A thick, tightly wrapped package tumbled from the bag to the floor. It created a hard thud behind the weight.

"What the fuck!" exclaimed Murder as he reached down to pick up the brick-like package.

He then took a look inside the bag and noticed four more bricks of the same.

This five keys of work here, he thought.

Upon a closer look of the bricks, he recognized the packages had the same type of distinct tape to secure them as the kilos he and Herb once had.

"This my shit! How the fuck did Quana get my shit?" Murder stated aloud.

His mother looked on at him in a questioning way.

Now Murder was really pissed at them both, his mother and his sister. He snatched his phone from his hip yet again to call Quana back. At the same time, he began to pillage through the closet looking for more. He knocked over everything in sight, the hanging clothes, the female shoe boxes, and the Jordan sneaker boxes Quana had re-situated the rolls of money in, similar to how Heeme had done things. Rolls of money the size of his fist dropped to the floor. Dude was so confused behind it all.

"Mom, go on in the back room for a moment, okay? We got something else going on now."

"Yeah. I see," Karen responded, then fast stepped on to the back.

Murder called Quana again. She answered.

"Bro, I'm almost—"

"Quana, where the fuck you get my bricks of product from?" he hissed in anger through gritted teeth.

"Huh?"

"These motherfuckin' bricks of work you got in your closet! Where you get it from? This my shit! I know you ain't stole from me, have you?!"

"Nah, bro! What make you think that? I yanked that shit from Heeme's spot right before I caught him and Tati together," Quana stated, speaking her truth in the matter.

"From Heeme's spot? Ok then. How the fuck did *that* nigga get his hands on my motherfuckin' material?"

"Look, I'll be there in a minute, bro. I'm not too far away."

"Well, you need to hurry up and get your ass here, because you got more than enough explaining to do now than anything!" Murder said, then ended the call.

Nearly ten minutes later, Quana was pulling up to her place. She hurried and got out the car, then speed-walked into the house. Her brother already had the five kilos and all the cash put away in one of the luggage bags that belonged to their mother. Quana was visibly shaken and her adrenaline continued to pump behind the shooting.

There, in the moment, they all had three intense situations to deal with. Murder took the initiative to air his out first.

"Quana, where the fuck did that nigga of yours, get my bricks of heroin from? That's my shit!" Murder spat, pointing at the bag for emphasis.

"That nigga been had that shit for a while now, bro. But since he wanna play games on my watch, him and that snake-ass bitch Tati, I'm keepin' all that shit I took from him! And that hunnid thousand dollars!" Quana spat.

"Quana, haven't you and Tatiana been hanging together since you picked her up from the bus station when she came back home?" asked Karen. She made her way to the living room where her two kids bickered.

Suddenly, Karen found her way in the clear from her son's wrath, due to the other two issues they had going on, Murder and Quana.

Quana didn't even bother to offer a reply to what her mother asked.

"Heeme and Tati sneaking around together on you?" Murder questioned.

"Yep! And I just got done blasting at them bitches too! Like whoa!" Quana spat.

"And you actually think that nigga trying to let this shit go without putting up a fight, Quana? Like, seriously, do you? Hell, for all we know, he probably on his way over here now." Murder made it make sense to his sister.

"I got something for that. And I know you do too," she let out, then brandished her gun in a gesture. She then raced to the bedroom to reload with another clip that was filled with hollow points. *Black Rhinos.*

Murder followed in her footsteps.

"You still not telling me how the fuck did that nigga Heeme get his hands on my work, Quana?" he continued to inquire.

"Bro, all I know is that the nigga came home one night with like ten or more bricks of that shit. We broke down a few of them and began to get money. After a few weeks of grinding only ounces at a time, we made a hunnid grand together. That's the money you got now. Then, that nut-ass nigga wanna start fucking around on me. With my own flesh and blood. Like I'm a dumb bitch or something. Ain't no telling how long the sneaky bitch Tati been fuckin' my man," Quana let out with an ungraceful tone to her voice. She went on. "And on top of that, how about the bitch, Tati, claimed to me that you paid her ten racks to off some pregnant bitch!" Quana let it spill.

Karen heard her and now looked on more intensely.

Murder had a petrified look about his face. He were at a complete loss for words, as he stood with both his eyes and mouth wide.

"Quana! How the fuck you know about that shit?" he uttered.

"Bro! The bitch gave me half the paper to play tag-along with her. That's how I know. And everything else to go along with that," Quana made him aware.

"Yo, you and me *both* gonna hurt that stupid bitch! Why the fuck would Tati let that out to anyone?" he questioned. Murder now had a serious situation on hand to deal with, in addition to the other issues he needed to resolve.

Quana's cell phone rang. There was a specific tone to play to let her know who it was calling. She answered. "What the fuck, nigga! It's over with dude! I'm keeping all that shit!" she spat at Heeme.

"Where the fuck is my money and my bricks of product, bitch? Huh?" Heeme returned fire. Apparently the gunshot wound he suffered wasn't that serious. He'd left West Philly and went to his pad. "And you missed me, bitch! But I promise to God, I won't miss you! You only grazed me on the shoulder!"

"I'll be sure not to miss next time. And that heroin product you had, I just found out it belonged to my brother, nigga! So, you already knowing how that's gotta go. You done really crossed the line now, pussy! Be ready to die," Quana threatened. Her tone of voice turned diabolical. Like it came from a pit of darkness only the devil was familiar with. She ended the call.

"Yo, listen. We gotta get the fuck outta here, y'all. And now! Quana, you and Mommy, take y'all asses down to Maryland and stay put until I tell y'all otherwise," Murder dictated.

"But, bro —"

"Don't fuckin' 'but bro' me! Just do what the fuck I tell you to, until I figure this shit out! A'ight!" Murder sharply responded. "Here!" He tossed Quana one of the rolls of money she previously had stashed. "Now you two get the fuck on down the highway. And be sure to call me when you get there. I've gotta go and track down that silly bitch and be sure she doesn't go too far in running her mouth with what she knows."

I might be able to use her to trap that nigga Heeme, Murder thought over.

The three of them all exited the house and got into their vehicles, headed two separate ways. Murder made the journey to his low-key home he owned in Bala Cynwyd to put away the kilos he now had and the money. The boy had more than enough on his plate to dispose of. However, the business he paid Tati to take care of, became top priority to deal with. If for whatever reason he didn't get a handle on it, the situation could become a virulent problem that might be hard to do away with later down the line.

Once Murder dropped off the bricks of heroin he had and half the money, he hit the road en route to D.C. to Charlotte's house. He brought along fifty thousand to have her keep for him. This was part of the plan all along he had in mind. To establish a deep level of trust with her and a bond like no other.

Little did he know, his whole world was on the verge of being turned upside down beginning that night, all behind a situation he had nothing to do with. Shit was crazy.

Chapter 6

Meanwhile ...

Over in West Philly, on the same block Tatiana lived, the homicide crime scene unit was present, and had a portion of the street roped off with yellow tape. An elderly woman and her young nine-year-old grandchild were struck by stray bullets while sitting in the living room of the senior citizen's home. The deadly lead missiles were fired from the barrel of Quana's Glock-17 at the time when she recklessly began cutting loose at Heeme and Tati.

The location of the house where the two victims were assaulted, leaving one dead and the other in critical condition, so happened to be directly in the path of which the assailant shot. Sixty-eight-year-old Ms. Susan Williams, suffered a wound to the right side of the head and was dead by the time paramedics and the cops arrived. The nine-year-old granddaughter of Ms. Williams was hit in the right leg. The bullet nicked the thigh bone as it passed through and entered her left leg. She would survive.

The lead homicide detective over the district, an Arnold Specter, was there to assess the situation. One of his underlings he supervised was there with him, Bernie Cochran. He also operated as a sidekick to Arnold, as the two often worked cases together. They had a good friendship as well.

Apparently, the nine-year-old was the one who called 9-1-1 for help. By the time medical attention got there, the little girl had lost a large amount of blood and had passed out. The 9-1-1 center was able to provide the correct address by the use of the home phone by the youngster. She was immediately taken to the hospital.

Upon obvious observance that Ms. Williams was no more, her body wasn't moved. The coroner was called, and he pronounced her dead.

Detective Specter and crew began conducting their investigation to determine what took place.

"I notice we've got three bullet holes here through the front window," Arnold said.

Anybody see or hear anything?"

"One of our investigators is over there now, having a talk with a female who claims to have seen and heard it all. We've recovered multiple spent shell casings from the middle of the street close to where the possible witness says she was situated," responded Cochran, the partner.

"Let's have a walk over there to see what all the witness may have to share with us," stated Arnold.

The two men then strutted in the direction where two uniformed police officers was jotting down notes of all the female related to them. It was evident by her appearance that she was a homeless drug addict. But nonetheless, to the cops, any witness is always credible until proven otherwise.

Arnold was the first to speak upon approaching. "Hello, ma'am. I'm Detective Arnold Specter of Philadelphia PD. If you will, could you recall for us all that you saw and all that you heard as it played out, please?" he politely asked.

The woman had an uncontrollable movement about her body, like maybe she was high or something to that effect. She was hyperactive and restless.

"Look, Officer. All I know is that I was over there," she pointed behind herself at an abandoned house that had plywood boards covering the windows, "seated on the back porch, minding my own business, doing what I do, and enjoying my coke. I sucked a dick to get ten dollars to buy it. Then all of a sudden, a small black shiny car pulled up and parked right here along the curb." They were three feet from where Quana had parked.

"What kind of small black shiny car was it?" Arnold asked.

"I don't know. A good-looking little sports car. One a person would drive who's not too rich and not too poor." Cochran wrote down what the woman said. "But the driver never got out of the car. They simply sat there for maybe thirty minutes. Like maybe they was waiting on somebody or checking out a house or something."

"And what were you doing the whole time the person in the car waited? For thirty minutes, as you say?"

"Shit, I continued to sit my little crackhead ass down on the porch in the alley and kept the hope in mind that whoever it was, may get out and give away testers of some new product they might've had. That they probably was looking to set up shop. It's usually how it goes the majority of the time, you know."

"But they never got out the car to do anything?"

"Nope. Not until a grayish car pulled up in front of that place there," she pointed at Tati's house, "to let out that pretty little mixed girl who not too long moved in."

"Pretty little mixed girl, you say? How you know she's biracial?" Arnold further inquired.

"It's because, I talk to her from time-to-time. And she feeds me and gives me money to run customers her way for the product she deals. It's not my type though. I like to get hyped. As you can tell," the woman stated.

All three white male officers then gave her the once over again and had a disgusted look about their faces.

"So the pretty little mixed girl is a crack dealer?" Cochran asked.

The woman then took her eyes from Arnold to place on his partner.

"I didn't say that. And no, she don't sell coke. The product she hustles is much more stronger than what I like. She moves *smack*. I love crack. Two totally different fortes."

Arnold was now eager to get the questions over and done with so they could move on from the so-called witness.

"Ok, so the person seated in the black sports car. Were they male or female? And what happened when the grayish car pulled up?" He posed a twofold question, attempting to speed up the process.

"Apparently, it had to be a female. I heard her yell out the word, 'Motherfucka,' to the top of her lungs from inside the car. And then, she just hopped out and began running towards the gray car, shooting at the mixed girl and some guy who was driving. The mixed chick took off running the other way. And the guy driving the gray car hit the gas coming this way. The girl doing the shooting took more shots as he passed. She then ran back to her car that was still parked, got in, and sped off. About five minutes passed and the pretty girl who lives there came back, got in her car, and left. Next thing I know, police sirens was heard. Then the ambulance pulled up to the house where y'all are now. What happened, somebody caught a stray or something?" the woman asked.

It was the third week in November and cool out that night. She had on multiple layers of thick clothes and a dark blue skull-cap.

The sidekick Cochran, wrote down everything the woman reported.

"Yeah. That's what happened. But it wasn't one person. There was two," Arnold stated. "One person is dead however."

"Damn! That's messed up there. Innocent people getting hurt or dying behind bullets that wasn't intended for them," the woman declared.

"From the looks of things, and from all you've stated to us, that may be what had happened. Thank you for your time.

And here is my card. I need for you to contact me whenever that 'pretty little mixed girl' comes back home who you say lives there," he pointed at Tati's house, "or if you spot that 'small black sports car' that the shooter was driving. Ok. take care!" Arnold lastly said, then promptly turned to walk away headed back to the house where the homicide unit was located, he and the two colleagues of his who were in his presence.

In theory, Detective Arnold concluded that all the homeless witness related to them checked out correctly. The forensics investigators stood in the spot where the shell casings were recovered and traced the projections of the bullets fired. Indeed, the three that went through the window of Ms. Williams' home, it was determined, came from the particular distance where it was now known the shooter recklessly took shots.

The official reports were written to reflect the investigation. And Arnold and partner Bernie Cochran, would return to Tatiana's house to attempt at asking her a few questions. No contact was made. She and Heeme was to go on about their business together, living from place to place, trying to figure out which way to go about bringing an end to the situations they faced, and how they were going to deal with Quana and Murder. At least, this was their plan. Both sides looked for a showdown to occur, in gunfire perhaps. The end of their story was to be drawn and written in blood.

Chapter 7

Herb set out to go and clip Ivan, on his murder-for-hire mission that his Russian counterpart Vladimir Bout had him on. He'd done the homework expected of him on the target, and now had a for sure way to hit his mark without Ivan's people knowing whom the real person was to give the order. The job had to be done properly to prevent retaliation. Ivan had powerful figure heads to back him. Therefore, Herb needed to balance his mode of attack. He couldn't be too professional about it nor too sloppy. A middle course had to be taken.

Vladimir made the fact known to Herb that Ivan had a mistress, whom he shared a two-year-old with. She was not from cultivated society as was Ivan, but rather of ordinary caste from Ukrainian immigrants in America. Very few knew of this affair, as Ivan kept things as private as possible. Ivan had Joliet and their child situated in a nice home over in Montgomery County, Norristown, Pennsylvania.

Joliet didn't get out too much as she understood her position with all she had going on with Ivan. This provided Herb an angle he could take so as to get the drop on dude. As a routine Ivan had created between the hours of 6:00 P.M. and 8:00 P.M. made this possible. Once his business was complete in downtown Philly, Ivan would travel to the home of the mistress to visit. And at times, he would enjoy meals with his secret family. Some days, he brought meals along with him, or either Joliet would order through DoorDash prior to Ivan arriving when he does daily. This would become how Herb could then get him, by posing as a delivery guy. Herb sat and watched the house for several days, leading up to the moment he'd decided to proceed.

It was a Friday. The first week in December. The sun had just set. The fall change of time was in full effect.

Herb had an outfit made to resemble the one DoorDash delivery people wore. The prepared meals he carried was pizza, wings, pasta, and steamed veggies. He had his hat pulled low in the event that Joliet or Ivan had any security features on the home. He approached the front door, food in hands, and pressed the doorbell. Ivan was known to order food in advance of him showing up. This was not unusual.

Joliet appeared and had a look through the peephole.

"Food delivery, ma'am," Herb politely spoke. He needed to win her trust.

Joliet thought nothing suspicious. This was the same as times past. Something Herb was sure to make note of throughout all the days he sat and watched the house.

"Is this a pre-order from Ivan again, sir?" she asked in her broken English and now opening the door.

"Yes ma'am. It is," Herb responded.

He had a getaway vehicle out front beside the curb of the home. His plan was well placed.

As soon as Joliet had the door opened far enough to where Herb had proper arm space, he viciously punched the thirty-year-old in the face, sending her to the floor. He then barged in and proceeded to hog-tie her with the black nylon laces and straps he had on hand, once he closed the door.

Traino emerged from his low position taken in the back seat of the car. He pulled off to await a phone call from Herb.

Once Joliet was thoroughly situated, Herb then dragged her up the stairs to the bedroom there. He placed her face down on the bed and tightly gagged her. The two-year-old was sound asleep, so there wasn't any need to attend to him.

Roughly forty-five minutes later, Ivan pulled up.

"Right on time," Herb said to himself. He'd taken cover in the hallway closet, the hallway that led to the bedroom where he had Joliet and the kid.

Ivan used his key to enter, locking the door behind himself. He then called out for Joliet in their native tongue as he made a pit stop by the kitchen. He proceeded up the stairs. The volume to the TV was up. A program on Lifetime, Joliot's favorite channel, played. Herb had left the door to the room slightly cracked. Ivan called out to her once more. He got no response. At the very moment he placed his hand on the doorknob to enter the room, Herb was easing out of the closet behind him.

The cold steel barrel of the .22 Ruger was firmly pinned to the back of Ivan's head. On instinct, he immediately threw his hands in the air to surrender.

"Uh!" Ivan exhaled from panic. He then wet his pants.

"I'm sorry, Ivan, this is the end for you. All I can promise is that I won't harm your mistress or your kid. Nonetheless, you . . . you gotta go," Herb stated in a disguising tone of voice.

Pop!

He put Ivan down with a head shot, point blank. Herb then sprinted to the bedroom to grab a pillow to muffle the additional shots that had to be administered.

Pop-Pop-Pop-Pop!

All head shots. Five in total to the dome. This was a statement killing. One intended to send a message.

Ivan never had the opportunity to look his killer in the eyes and come to see whom it was who got him. He wasn't allowed to turn to face his killer. And so, he was no more. His time had expired.

Chapter 8

To prevent the U.S. Attorney's office from pursuing prosecution on him and sending him off to prison for the remainder of his natural life, Ralphie Arroyo made the decision to cooperate with the federal government. He was now in the process to assist them in their attempts to take down his leader and drug supplier, Felipe Valdez.

Ralphie spoke on all he knew under oath of perjury to them related to the day-to-day operations of Felipe. He also provided names of other dealers he had knowledge of along the network. Indeed, the feds felt they'd found the weakest link in the crew and began to utilize him like a dishrag, and wring out as much dirty water as they could, while doing the dishes in the underworld kitchen of vice.

Ralphie spoke loosely to his interviewers and began to piece together the puzzle for them, so as to give them a better picture of how Highway operated.

"So, Arroyo, give us the complete line-up of the chain-of-command of the *Puerto Rican Dragons, aka, PRDs* have in place. The group you're a member of?" asked Felicia.

This time, it was her and another colleague having a stab at Ralphie. He was being held in the FDC Downtown Philly on 6th Street and Market.

"I've told you. There's Felipe, who is the head. And then there's his brother Uriel, who's—"

"Uriel!" Felicia retorted. "You've never mentioned that name to us."

"Yeah. well. I'm doing so now, I thought, ain't I?" Ralphie fired back sarcastically.

Felicia began to write down the new name in her notepad.

"You better not be bullshitting us, Arroyo. Or else, out the home goes Momma. And into Children and Youth goes your little ones. You got that!" declared William Flannigan, the AUSA assisting alongside Felicia.

"Look, man! Once more. The line-up is this. You got Highway at the top—"

"Highway!" Flannigan cut in to say.

"That's Felipe Valdez," Felicia informed.

"Gotcha!" Flannigan concurred, then raised his tall lanky frame ramrod again and ran his fingers from both hands through his bushy top hair.

"Continue, Ralphie," Felicia instructed.

"As I was saying. It's Highway, Uriel, then me along the food chain. And with me being third in line, I don't believe you would want anyone lower than me, now would you?" Ralphie stated.

"You got that part correct. And we see you're getting the hang of how this agreement works," spoke Flannigan once more. He appeared to have a disdainful attitude towards Spanish street thugs for all his reasons he deemed feasible.

Years prior, Flannigan's one and only older brother was robbed and murdered by a Puerto Rican dope peddler, and he'd never fully healed from his grief. Not to mention, the fact that Flannigan was a staunch MAGA Republican advocate and overly infatuated with the then president of the United States, Donald J. Trump. He'd voted for the guy and embraced the proposed idea of a wall along the southern border. Flannigan saw all Spanish people as one and the same. They were everything to him that Donald Trump say they were.

"What about any connections outside the Puerto Rican Dragons that Valdez may have? We're interested in these as well," Felicia spoke.

"And I'm sure you are. I'm here to tell y'all anything you wanna know, to have you people back off from bothering my mother and kids," Ralphie stated.

"We like the sound of that. Now talk. Our agreement depends on your level of cooperation. Don't lose the thought of that. Not for once. Because the moment you do, the rug will be snatched from under you," Felicia made their informant totally aware.

Ralphie smiled at her comment. He then continued to speak.

"Thanks for reminding me, sweetheart. But anyway. Highway—"

Felicia cut his words short. "This interview is being monitored and recorded. So be sure to mention that Felipe Valdez is indeed 'Highway' as well. Okay?" she uttered.

"No problem. Felipe Valdez, aka 'Highway,' has ties to a black guy who's a distro as well. Some high-profile guy they call 'Mayor' or something like that. They're both being supplied numerous kilos by a Colombian Cartel chief. That's all I know so far on that."

"Would this Colombian Cartel chief have a name you know of?" Felicia asked.

"All I know is that Highway, or Valdez rather, refers to him by his initials. He only shows up here in Philly maybe three to four times out the year," Ralphie mentioned. "The initials 'G.R.'"

Alvarez and Flannigan were already in possession of this information and immediately went to their notepads to confirm things.

The initials "G.R." referred to none other than Gustavo Ruiz. The two prosecutors knew this to be true. However, they kept that knowledge to themselves and gave no indication to Ralphie that they were aware, although he was telling the truth.

The interview continued, but now in a different direction.

"Tell us more about this black distro Valdez has an acquaintance with. What do you have on him?" Felicia urged Ralphie with her question.

Her intention was to know all she could learn about those under Ruiz, then later utilize that information to lead them to a smoking gun perhaps.

"As I've said, all I know is that he's some type of high-profile figure in the city. He moves a lot of weight. And doesn't really have to get his hands dirty. I remember a time before when Highway had me and his brother deliver five kilos each to two of the workers of this black distro I'm telling you about. Uriel said he knew one of them from around the neighborhood in North Philly. Some badass with an attitude everybody called by the name '*Murder.*' He's known for being trigger happy from what I've heard," Ralphie related.

"You and Uriel delivered five kilos each of what type of product to the two guys?" asked Flannigan.

"That's a logical answer, there. What type of product did y'all catch me with? It was heroin. That's the only drug we all sell up and down the network. Nothing else," Ralphie answered the question put to him.

This turned out to be the third time that the prosecutors had heard the name "Murder" mentioned to them but hadn't been able to identify any person of interest. The first time this occurred was when the missing confidential informant Montez Shaw, aka "Duck," and his girlfriend brought it to their attention. The second time, Duck's sister stated the name to them as a potential person who may have wanted her brother harmed behind issues within the street life they lived. And now, for the third time, they had the name "Murder" tossed their way by Ralphie.

No one in the office of the US Attorney knew who this mysterious "Murder" guy was. This complicated their agenda to pursue the potential intended targets they could take aim at and nab. The hope was that each one they would arrest, would give up all they knew about Ruiz, rather than risk going to trial and receiving long sentences in prison.

***

Not long before the day, the Philadelphia U.S. Attorney's office was contacted by the Washington D.C. office regarding loose statements made by someone who was part of the Witness Protection Program. A new investigation was opened on this particular individual. And during a day enjoyed at the spa by this female, along with her friend, an in-depth conversation between the two, produced more than enough evidence to establish probable cause to enable further investigation. Specifically, on the names of the people brought to their attention by the candid and loose speech between the two women.

John Fletcher, the U.S. Attorney there in Philadelphia, was intent on utilizing the intel provided to his office from the D.C. prosecutors. To make matters more of an advantage for Fletcher, the wife's name of a city council member was mentioned as being the friend of the person who the federal government provided protection. And at the time when Alvarez and Flannigan interviewed Ralphie, the third time, Fletcher was sure to tune in. He wanted to cross-reference the notes on file with the information provided by his counterparts down in the nation's capital, the newly revealed material from an already complying informant. Everything matched up.

Fletcher didn't want to, but in order to protect the reputation and integrity of the Philadelphia city board councilmen, he had no choice but to make it known that the mentioned name of a man who was possibly a distro for an international drug trafficker, was an elected official, Major Appleton.

Everything was all speculation at this point, until corroborated with facts and evidence. But the question still remained. Who was this "Murder" guy? How does he factor into the grand scheme of things? And how might his true identity be made known? Being that his name had been mentioned on numerous occasions, and by multiple people, Fletcher figured if they were to find out who he was and grab him, he'd lead them to the activities of Major and get them one step closer to Ruiz.

Fletcher and crew now had an abundance of material to work with and began putting together a potential prosecution package for the whole network in the Philly area. From Gustavo Ruiz on down. An epic battle between the two empires loomed. On one end, you have a unit that was presumed good. While on the other, there was one presumed evil. Nonetheless, there was evil inside the circle of good, a mole who worked for Ruiz. And good inside the circle of evil, the wives and girlfriends of the drug dealers. One team had to win and one had to lose. The war on drugs raged on.

Chapter 9

Murder packed bags and headed to D.C. again to lay low for a few weeks due to the issues now affecting him with Heeme. He wasn't able to gain any level of comfort in moving about in Philly until the people hired to do the job managed to track dude down and kill him. Murder's security and that of his sister, was now top priority, and he was restless until the fact was to be made known to him that the threat was no more. With the moves he was making and the large quantity of product that had to be sold, he didn't need no little flea of a nigga gunning for him with each corner to be turned. Especially not behind some relationship drama.

The issue wasn't that he was afraid of Heeme. No! Dude was far from that. He just had too much shit going on in his rise to be a boss than to risk being shot at or worse, killed. So the easiest thing for him to do was to simply put out the hit and resolve the situation this way.

His intention was to be between the hotel in D.C., Charlotte's house, and at his mom's home in Maryland. And only go to Philly on a need-be basis to handle his business, then be gone. He figured it shouldn't take his hitters too long to get Heeme. Maybe this was true. Maybe it wasn't. However, he was super determined to get Heeme. And likewise, Heeme was super determined to get him. Quana as well.

***

That night when Murder first got to D.C. following Quana shooting at the two, he made a stop by Charlotte's house. They had a few things to talk about.

"So, what brings you here on such short notice, Barry?" Charlotte asked as the two were in the privacy of her bedroom.

Charlotte's daughter, Ni'Asia, was in her bedroom completing homework and listening to music. The time was just past 11:00 P.M. She liked the idea of her mother having a man around the house for a change. Charlotte's energy was different. And she allowed the young girl the pleasure to be in her own world and to do her own thing uninterrupted.

"Well, I can't lie to you. I've got to be honest," he began. "I hated the distance between us. And I believe I'm ready for us to move in together. Ten months is a long enough time for us to get familiar with one another for this to happen. Also, my sister had a problem with her boyfriend that led to a violent altercation," he related.

Charlotte jarred her head at the mention of a domestic dispute that resulted in violence. She had flashbacks to the past when Reign Man used to beat on her and all that resulted from that.

"Quana! Oh, my! Is everything being worked out?"

It became evident that Charlotte's level of anxiety had risen.

"I can't say so just yet. We're working on it. It shall be soon," Murder responded, with the thought of the three hitters he had on the lurk around town looking for Heeme.

"I'm afraid to even ask, what happened?"

"Typical shit that goes on when a good girl don't wanna let go of a thug they have as a boyfriend. Chaos will always follow, leaving the two to go through a rough and ugly break up. In this situation, Quana's lame-ass boyfriend decide he wanted to sneak around and begin fuckin' with a cousin of ours. Quana eventually caught 'em. She messed around and got so pissed that she pulled her gun and shot at both of them fools."

"Oh-my-fucking-God! That's a lot! I'm sure that whoever the boyfriend is really wished he hadn't did that now, doesn't he?" she retorted, while at the same time, thinking over the situation on how she'd come to know her ex-boyfriend was sleeping around with her cousin, and the feeling she experienced. Charlotte wanted to shoot and kill somebody herself while heated in the moment.

"I'm more than sure he does. And now, me and my boys gotta be sure to handle everything before shit really gets outta control. I don't have the time nor the patience to go back and forth with dude about this. So, the best thing I knew to do was to get me and my sister out of the way until things die down and peace is re-established."

"That makes sense. Because ain't no telling what the boyfriend is subject to, but that goes both ways," Charlotte said on the matter. "So, where's Quana now?"

"She's over in Maryland. At our mom's place."

"Oh. So your mother lives in Maryland?"

"Yep. We'll go over to meet her one day soon, if you like. But before that, I've got a few problems with her I've gotta work out. I don't care to speak on right now," Murder stated.

At the mention of his mother, he'd brought Charlotte's own to her mind, and the phone conversation the two had not long before the day. There was a need for Charlotte to contact her mother again soon, so that Ni'Asia and her grand mom could have the opportunity to speak with one another. Charlotte's mother never called back that day, as she felt that if Charlotte really wanted her to speak with the young one, she'd be the one to call again, as she had already. Also, Charlotte needed to be provided with Shug's information to reach out to her. There was a lot of explaining that needed to be done.

Charlotte continued to speak. "Well look, Barry. You and I are definitely headed in the right direction, as I wouldn't want what we are establishing to go no other way. And you are more than welcome to stay here for as long as you like. No need for a hotel," Charlotte said, then grabbed the extra set of house keys from the dresser drawer and gave them to Murder.

"Here you go. These are yours. You can come and go as you so please. Besides, me and my daughter can get used to a man being around here for a change. One whom I truly know has our best interest at heart. And doesn't mean us any harm in the least," Charlotte expressed, then held up her hand that had the ring on it he'd bought for her.

They both smiled ecstatically. He loved to see her happy as she was in that moment.

"Thanks, Charlotte. You're the best. I brought something else along with me too. I'm gonna need for you to keep this here between us, ok?" he said to her.

"And what might that be?" She was eager to know. Charlotte loved the surprises Murder had to offer. But then, she had a second thought. Murder was in D.C. to avoid trouble with someone. And felt he was about to equip her with a gun. Or have one of his boys he utilized for security, stand guard to protect her. A concerned look came about from the second thought.

"Relax, sweetie. I wasn't talking about a gun or a grenade, Charlotte," he uttered, making humor of his reply.

Murder then grabbed the straps to the Gucci backpack he had and tossed it to Charlotte.

"A special gift from me to you. I'm sure you're gonna love that too," he stated then smiled.

Charlotte felt the weight of the backpack then had a peep inside. She was greeted by multiple, tightly rolled, hundred-dollar-bills secured with colorful rubber bands.

"And what am I supposed to do with all this?" she asked with a huge smile about her face. "Go on a spending spree with it? Exercise some retail therapy? That is an actual thing, you know."

Charlotte appeared to be joking about it. But at the same time, loved the idea of it all.

"It depends on what type of shopping spree you're looking to go on. As a matter of fact. Let's play a little game. If I was to put a hundred thousand dollars in your hands, that right there," he pointed to the backpack, "what would you do with it? How would you spend it?" He wanted to know.

If Charlotte was to correctly answer, and in a way to appease him, he might do just that. Give it all to her. What the hell. It was free money anyway. And besides that, he'd not long before gotten supplied with double the amount in heroin product that he usually took on. So, the loss of the fifteen kilos was made up for with the amount received of the new shipment. Not to mention the fact that Herb was half in on the fifteen stolen. Everything was good.

"Well, the first thing I'd do is, make a large deposit down on a new home. Put maybe seventy-five K towards that. Then I'd take ten thousand and add to the funds I've already got in place to go towards my daughter's college tuition money. I'd then take ten thousand more to start a small business with. And the last five, I'd do some shopping with it. But not spend it all. But back to the house."

Murder kept silent and listened to her very attentively.

"I would like to find one in Philadelphia, in your city, because that's where I'd love to relocate to. That way, we'd be closer in every regard, if we're really gonna do this. And the sisterhood I'm looking to be a part of, under Miss Lori Appleton," she managed to sneak in what her true intentions were, "could take place in a more effective way. But to answer your question specifically, that's exactly what I'd do with a hundred grand," Charlotte stated confidently. "Did my response impress you?"

"No doubt, it did. Especially the part about you wanting to move to Philly. How much truth is it to that?" Murder wanted to know.

"There's a lot of truth to that. Because that's exactly what I wanted you to hear to know what it is that I really want," she replied, then eased closer to him atop the bed where they sat.

"Sweet Barry," she let out then kissed him. "If you let me."

They kissed once more.

Charlotte had more to relate. "Also, Barry, Lori gave me a call. The both of us are drawing closer as friends. She adores me and I really adore her. And I've been offered the opportunity to join her social circle to potentially become a member. But I told her straight up that I'll have to check with my man first to see how you feel about all this. I'm hoping my timing is good."

"Yeah, you're good. Everything is cool. And I promise you, once I resolve these little issues I got going on at the moment, we can then begin buying a home together. One in Philly. Just please, let me square things away first, please. That's my word. A'ight?" Murder said, providing Charlotte the assurance she wanted from him. In words at least.

Charlotte then took a look down at the backpack that was loaded with bread.

"And my hundred grand?" she uttered, then tapped the side of the thick leather Gucci item.

"Oh, yeah. That. It's not a hundred thousand there. It's more like one-twenty. It's all yours. Keep it. As long as you and Ni'Asia are all mine. That y'all belong to me. You're my responsibility. Because that's what I'm ready for. A family, Charlotte. That's what I want," Murder gracefully expressed his most sincere desires. He poured out his heart to her and was true about it.

Charlotte smiled from ear to ear. It appeared as big as the Amazon logo. She leaned in again for more tender kisses, followed by a passionate tango of the tongues.

The two continued to converse over their future together and lay in the plans for the living arrangements they had in mind. Charlotte then called out for her daughter to come and join them as they talked further.

Little did Ni'Asia know at the time she had no reason to fear losing contact and friendship with Imani's daughter, Farrah. Both of their mothers were already in agreement for a separation of the two to not occur. As soon as the first was to move, was situated—in this case Charlotte—the other, which would be Imani, would soon follow with the assistance of the lead person. Everything was already established in that regard.

Throughout the conversation of the three, Charlotte clearly explained to her daughter whom Barry was to them from that point moving forward. Charlotte then left the two to themselves to further become acquainted. She made her way to the shower. But, before doing so, she grabbed hold of the backpack that had her cash in it and went into the walk-in closet. She had a mini-safe located inside. Charlotte put her money away then went to wash up.

Ni'Asia took Murder by the hand and escorted him to her room. Her personal space was beautifully decorated in her favorite colors. There was pink, purple, violet, and periwinkle. Charlotte was sure to provide the youngster with the essential latest in devices. She had a computer, a tablet, and a smartphone. The mother and daughter favored Samsung culture more so than that of Apple. Ni'Asia did her homework on her tablet and asked Barry to check over everything for her. He did so and the two continued to talk more.

Charlotte came out of the bathroom, located in her bedroom. She was covered in a thick terrycloth pink robe. The garment matched her favorite brand of soap, Caress. Most women make the same connection, bath essentials with towels, washcloths, and underclothing.

"Barry!" Charlotte called out for him.

He left Ni'Asia to herself and made his way back to the mother. The little girl put her earbuds back in and got back to listening to music.

Murder stepped into Charlotte's room once more and quickly took notice of the stage that was being set in her domain. The energy she gave off displayed that of a woman who was healing properly. Absolutely nothing pieces a broken woman back together again as does good dick and kind treatment, the two things Murder had already provided.

Murder closed the door behind himself and locked it. He then stood with both hands on his hips and took in all the beauty he looked upon. Charlotte had already peeled off the robe and was now putting on music from her playlist on her phone. The sensual and intoxicating voice of Dej Loaf emitted from the phone. Charlotte began to snake her body to the beat in an erotic format. To Murder, there was something more appealing about the appearance of her body in that instance than it was the first time he'd seen her naked. This was probably due to her total compliance with the workout regime she now had, and a recent color tattoo of a heart and rose just inside her inner left thigh, and the inclusion of a few piercings of the nipples of her breasts and one of the navel. She had it going on.

Charlotte grooved her body in a three-hundred-sixty-degree rotation slowly. Murder's erection bulged inside the thin material fabric Jordan sweatsuit he had on. Charlotte caught a glimpse and really began to put on for him. She then paused and grabbed a bottle of lotion from atop the dresser. She put a nice sized amount into the palm of her hands, clasped them together and went into a circular motion clockwise. Charlotte slathered the moisturizer all about her body then slid both hands down her legs while bending at the waist enticingly. Her backside was facing Murder's direction. The love box that sat below jumped out at him from underneath. He damn near lost all control of himself in the moment.

A thought came to Murder's mind. He knew Charlotte was deeply into all things health and medicine. She didn't play around about unprotected sex. And unfortunate for him, no matter how bad he yearned for the pussy, he didn't have any condoms on hand to accommodate the occasion. He'd shown up on short notice, catching her off guard in the process. However, something would have to give. And he had something he intended to present to her to make the situation favorable for him. More than likely, Charlotte would go for it.

Murder rushed in on Charlotte, locking his arms around her waist, and began to ravish her with wet kisses all about her neck, cheekbone, and breast area. It was as if dude had become possessed by a love bug or something. Her sex appeal had infected him. Or was it simply a case of lust and desire?

"Barry! Wait! Hold up a moment, please. I really want to get to this part with you. But I don't have any condoms. What about you? And I'm sure you already know how protective I am of my body and life," she said to him in an emphatic tone.

"You're right. I need to slow it down. And no. I don't have any condoms either. And I'm just like you when it comes to that. Protective of my body and life. That's the reason I brought this with me," he responded, then made his way to the backpack he had the money in and put his hands on a piece of paper to show her.

Twice a year, Murder goes to see his doctor for a physical. Just two days before, he'd done so, and had a printout with certifications to prove the results. He was NEGATIVE in all the categories related to infectious diseases. Dude was in good health.

"Here you go," he said and presented his paperwork to her. I'm sure you're familiar with it all." He then smiled at her. Causing Charlotte to do the same.

She took a good look at the document. Indeed it was official.

"So I guess we're at the phase now to where we can consider eliminating condoms then, aren't we?" she responded, half-jokingly and half being very sincere. She continued. "Look, I'mma go along with the flow, because I'm never the one to spoil a good thing. I just want you to be sure that you pull out of me at the point of reaching your climax, ok? Because I can't let you get me pregnant your very first time getting the pussy," Charlotte let out with a smile. "We've gotta work our way up to that point. But don't worry. I won't have you waiting too long."

Her sensational smile was still on display.

In that instance, a thought passed through her mind. One of a remark that her daughter Ni'Asia made to her. She'd mentioned to her mother that she wanted a sibling. A sister. And she didn't want to get too far up in age before her mom provided her with one. No doubt, Charlotte wanted the same. But the process wasn't going to begin that night.

"Don't worry, sweetie. I will. But to be honest, I don't know how long I could hold back from finally being able to shoot up your club. My shit strong too," Murder responded. He had a genuine level of wit to his words and caused her to continue smiling.

The two embraced and began to kiss once more. Murder didn't waste any more time to get naked as she was. He was primed up and ready to put in work. He gently took hold onto both her shoulders and turned her to face in the opposite direction. Dude wanted to pop things off in this area with her in doggystyle, and then later, transition into other things. He was now there in her life and home like he wanted to be. And also, had a key to come and go how he saw fit. Therefore, he was able to take all the time he wanted. It was all good from that day moving forward.

Charlotte took the initiative to bend over on her own and palm the floor with both hands. Murder then began to situate the head of his manhood at the entrance of her love garden. He then penetrated and began to do all he had longed to do in his mind, fuck her ever-loving brains out of her head and make her say his name until she could no longer. He was going to make her sing like an opera star would, to impress the pope.

Murder and Charlotte fucked repeatedly all throughout the night. He kept his word and didn't release a load inside of her. She caught the first one he let go with her mouth. The next two was on her belly and on her ass-cheeks. They really had a good time pleasing one another. It was magical.

Chapter 10

Heavy tension between the top two Spanish drug enterprises in Philly was on the verge of creating a war. The Latin Kings and the Puerto Rican Dragons now hated each other and didn't want to have any type of sit-down to resolve their issues. The Latin Kings pointed the finger at the other in blame for Gourdo's death. And the PRDs felt disrespected behind the accusations leaving Highway to hold back on supplying the now leader over them with the product of the new batch. Also, it didn't help the situation in the least with Gourdo's brother 'Premo, coming off to Highway as a reckless hot head who had no business about himself, and didn't truly understand how things worked along the network.

The initial meeting between the two was a disaster. And with Highway being back in power with his product, he utilized the kilos of heroin as a weapon to generate money and buy more guns to ensure that he and the group he represented, remain the strongest. At least on the Spanish side of things.

'Premo proved to be more than the hot head, business-like dumbo Highway made him out to be. Since the killing of his sibling, he'd tightened the ranks of his crew and did away with those perceived to be weaklings. He also held onto a bit of information that would help him gain an advantage over Highway. He'd learned that Highway had a couple of soldiers who'd flipped and became informants.

They were ratting to the local police and the feds. And with that being so, it was only a matter of time before the PRDs would be replacing their leader. Highway was doing too much on both ends.

***

Highway Valdez hosted a party to honor himself and the day he was initiated as a Puerto Rican Dragon. Each year since, he has celebrated the anniversary. He rented a popular strip club in North Philly for the yearly occasion. It was called "Night on Broadway" located on Broad and Olney near the main transit bus terminal. The place was heavily populated with mostly Spanish speaking patrons. Puerto Rican folks from all about the city and surroundings.

Ralphie Arroyo was set free by the feds to serve their purpose. They forced him to wear a wire and gather additional information. He was a trusted worker of Highway and part of the security team closest to him. The feds knew this as well. This was mainly why he was ordered to be wired. The gun and drug charges he faced was temporarily suspended. He had to do the work they wanted him to do first. Their plan was working.

Highway had a secret no one knew, other than himself and those he enjoyed doing what he did with. He favored Cuban females over Puerto Ricans. And he liked to be fully penetrated in his anus with a dildo while having sex with them. He was bisexually curious.

Amongst the dancers there that night, one was Cuban. Her features were strong yet feminine, her skin was a darker shade than the typical Puerto Rican Latina. Her breasts, thighs, and butt, resembled Negroid genetics Cubans carry, and there was something much more appealing about this one in terms of taboo that stood out to Highway. He instantly took notice.

The female purposely put herself in Highway's eyesight and mystically grooved to the music to appease. It was as if she knew exactly who Highway was and only sought out his attention. She eased closer within his arm's reach. He was mesmerized at her energy and wanted to experience more of it. He motioned with his index finger for her to come closer. She followed his command. His security men was told by him to stand down. They all were in the VIP section.

The female now stood face-to-face with him. She whispered into his ear. It had to be something lovely to cause him to want more of her actions performed. She then kissed him on his clean-shaven cheekbone. The two walk hand-in-hand from VIP to the private booth area in back of the club. She led the way. Once inside, the female straddled Highway for a lap dance as he was situated on the love seat. He forgot about everything and gave into the moment.

Once fully into things, the female reached above her head into the bun of hair she had to pinch hold of whatever it was she was eager to get her hands on. Highway's head was tilted back and his eyes closed. He didn't notice a thing that she was doing.

Suddenly, Lulianna, the sister of Lucy and Hitter herself, began to viciously stab Highway with a thin, sturdy eight-inch ice pick she'd used to pin her hair. She whacked away with the bony, sharp pointed object, hitting him in the neck, chest, and torso. A nerve along the bone of his neck was pricked, causing him to lock up in paralysis and he couldn't move to fight back. He wasn't able to yell out for help either. He slumped over onto the seat. Blood oozed slowly from the wounds he suffered. His life was seeping away.

Lulianna began to climb over the padded wall that separated the booth they were in. No one occupied the other one she intended to make her escape from. The thick swath of a wig was snatched from her head to reveal the natural low cut. It was dyed red. She tossed her weapon under the seat in the booth where she now stood, removed the two-piece she had on but still covered in another of a different color, then nonchalantly walked out. Passing Highway's two bodyguards, who stood twenty feet from the booth they'd originally entered. She went through the crowd on the dance floor, up the short flight of stairs that led from the below ground level den of the club and out the door, never to be seen again. No one took notice of anything. Lulianna had just hit one of the biggest street drug kingpins in all of Philly. Highway's security would have hell to pay once the attack came to the light. Ralphie happened to be one of the two who stood close by at the time the hitter struck.

It was Dark Skinned Jermaine who'd called the hit. His process of elimination was rolling again. He knew that by the time he was to exit prison, he had to get rid of all those who numbered along the network Ruiz supplied, so as to prevent any threat that lay along his pathway to power. That included Murder as well. He was still a piece to be reckoned with on the board of street chess which they played. With him being far more difficult piece to deal with, the mind state and movement of Murder, could be attributed to that of a knight piece, as opposed to that of Highway's, who resembled the rook, with its predictable up-and-down, side-to-side form of motion. Nonetheless, Murder was someone who could still get got.

***

The sexual affair Heeme and Tatiana began was nowhere near at a point of coming to an end. Even with the fact of the two putting their lives on the line to be with one another, it only motivated them that much more to go harder with what they had going on, now that what was in the dark had come to the light, literally by the flash from Quana's gun that is.

Quana was so pissed and hellbent on vengeance, that she didn't think twice before doing what she had. Her crazy ass narrowly escaped a "quadruple" homicide and didn't even know it. Tragically, an elderly grandmother did lose her life. And the police were determined to pin a murder rap on somebody. They looked to do so in due time.

Heeme and Tati met back up that same night and returned to the hotel they'd been in earlier in the evening. The leeway to spend quality time together wasn't an issue any longer. A deep conversation was begun to discuss the matter.

"Heeme! Please tell me what you plan to do about that crazy bitch, Quana! Because I don't intend to be getting shot at every time I decide to come out of hiding," Tati uttered to him. Her anxiety ran rampant.

"I can't even begin to tell you what I'mma do with that bitch. But I do know I've gotta do something. That bitch is a lunatic!" responded Heeme.

"I don't really think the bitch gonna continue going 'scorched earth' on us like that. I've got too much on her. And her brother knows her fucked up behavior could be bad for business. I'm more than sure he'll talk some degree of sense into her at some point. Then, she'll have to calm down. Mark my words."

"Yeah, but what if she doesn't? What if she sees you and me together again and goes off for a second time? Because I don't plan to stop fuckin' with you. And we're not gonna continue to run and hide in order to enjoy what we've started. Not me. Not from no bitch! Quana got me fucked up!" Heeme vented.

"So why won't you simply tell her you don't wanna fuck with her no more, and that it's you and me now? She can't force you to be with her if you don't want to." Tati's solution was a logical one. But she still didn't seem to understand her cousin. Shaquana Fredricks, wasn't no logical female. Not in the least.

"Tatiana, I don't think you get it. Thing's not that simple fuckin' with Quana. Period. Like . . . she not long ago tried to assassinate us! Don't you get it! To her, I'm to kill or die for! Ain't no other way than those two!

Tati thought carefully over his words before offering a response.

"Well, truth be told, Heeme, you do got some good dick on you. I can't lie about that. But goddamn! She taking shit *too* far!"

"Shit! Who you telling! I know that now! I always thought she was just talking shit for the fuck of it. But that psycho bitch dumped a whole clip at you and me both! And I ain't never been shot at that many times," Heeme stated.

He carried an expression about his face as if he gave glory to God for blessing him in not being killed.

"I ain't never been shot at in no point of my life!" Tati came back with. "Much less, that many times! But I know what I can do. I can have her brother Barry, make her fall back. Because I've got something on him as well."

"You talking 'bout that shit you and Quana did for him to that pregnant female, ain't you?"

"Heeme, how the fuck you know about that?" Tati said in outburst. She now began to panic.

"Tati, Quana used to tell me everything. And when I say everything, I mean *everything*. I had it to where I used to have her equip me with all kinds of information on street shit. If you only knew how scared she was that I'd someday leave her. I utilized that to my advantage."

"So you was able to control her based on the good dick game you got on you?"

"If you wanna put it that way, then yeah. And don't be acting like you don't know how long I've been fucking with Quana. She just recently became too much to deal with. Then you dropped back in and provided me with some hope. Quana don't want shit outta life but to be stuck under me and in the streets with her brother. If only you knew how many times I'd tried to get her ass to go and enroll in a school so she could learn something, and we could possibly start a business together. Nothing worked. And I got tired of that shit quite frankly. But you . . . you different. You want something outta life. You wanna go places. You wanna experience different shit. You wanna be somebody. I can really fuck with that. Like for real, for real, I can. And that's why I'm here with you now," Heeme said. He relayed his honest thoughts and truest desire.

Tati smiled like she never had before. Heeme's words made her feel good. Most dudes she'd dealt with in her past had a hard time expressing the gentleman side of themselves. Not Heeme. He was the type who delighted in doing so. He was always willing to prove that he was much more than just an average street nigga of his generation. It was the sensible side he possessed that made him a bit vulnerable to the females he was with. A special quality that Quana developed an infatuation with. And at this particular point, her cousin who stole her man, seemed to be doing the same thing.

"You can really fuck with me, huh? I like the sound of that. But here's what I really need you to do. I need for you to fuck with me in a way that we both can win. Together. Because everybody else before you just made it all about them. They used me only as a piece of ass when they wanted to fuck. I hated that shit! But Heeme, if we're gonna do this, how are we gonna get to the money as a team? My money is low now," Tati said.

"No need to worry about that. I'm a 'Jones' baby. JBM to the death of me in this new millennium. My people still strong in the game. They gonna be sure I'm good. And, I've got a couple dollars of my own to play with. So, we good. I just gotta be sure to get my motherfuckin' bricks of dope and my money back from that bitch you got for a cousin! She stole my shit! Look!" Heeme said, then showed Tati the photos Quana sent him.

"Wow! Just fuckin' wow! That's all I can say," she remarked. "How much is that? Money and the other stuff?"

"That's a hunnid thousand dollars and five bricks of heroin."

"What the fuck! That's enough to get a bitch killed! Quana done went too goddamn far!"

"This is something serious," Heeme responded. "Enough to push me to the point to where I'm gonna have that bitch killed!" he spat further.

"Well, she made it this way. She attacked first," said Tati.

"And I know exactly how to hit back," Heeme declared.

The two continued to talk and make plans on how they was to move together as a couple. They seemed to be determined to make a name for themselves one way or the other.

***

Two Days Later …

Tatiana received a call from someone there was a need to have a conversation with, before the problems she had to deal with became too much. The caller was her notorious cousin, Murder. She was reluctant to take the call at first. But knew there may be consequences to her actions if she hadn't.

"Hello!" she answered.

"Tati! What the—"

"Look, Barry! Don't start with me about Quana! Because I ain't tryna hear that shit! A'ight? I'm dead ass!" She cut his words off.

"Bitch, who the fuck you think you talking to like you crazy! You better get a handle on that shit, Tati! ASAP!" he thunderously let out.

"I'm just saying, Barry—"

"You ain't saying shit! *I'm* doing all the talkin' over here! Get that part straight first! Then move on to the other shit!" Murder spat.

Tati didn't say another word. She knew better and simply kept quiet.

"Now, look. What the fuck you doing putting Quana in our business? Never mind the bullshit y'all got going on over a piece of dick! But why the fuck would you be so stupid to do other than what I paid you to do by yourself? You wasn't supposed to let nobody else know anything about that." Murder demanded straight answers.

"Barry. I needed a helping hand to do the job, and Quana was the only one I knew I could trust on something like that."

"So you mean to tell me, you can trust her to tag along with you to catch a body, but she can't trust your ass two minutes around her dude? Is that what the fuck you telling me?" he barked.

"It ain't even like that with me and Heeme, on some for real shit."

"Bitch, stop lying to me! How the fuck it ain't like that with you two, when you got Quana blasting at you motherfuckas' like she *Yosemite Sam* or somebody over there in West Philly! Now try to explain that shit to me! Y'all provoked her."

Tati was at a loss for words. She did as before and kept quiet, to prevent from getting angry or from causing Murder from doing so. She knew how he could get.

"Tati, ain't no excuses for that shit. And I don't know how, but the nigga you and Quana beefing over, happened to get his hands on my motherfuckin' dope! The both of them owe me some motherfuckin' answers! They definitely do."

"Well, that part I don't know nothing about," Tati responded.

"I didn't say you did. I said, they owe me some answers. And I intend to get them too. Quana not off the hook about that all because she's my sister. Fuck no! And in fact, she's the one more to blame about certain shit. But the reason I called you is because I plan to get you two stupid cunts together, so we can dead all the bullshit y'all got going on over some nut-ass nigga! Long before that shit cause all of us some problems. Problems like a motherfuckin' murder charge behind a dead pregnant chick! So truth be told, I highly advise you to get your mind right and be ready to meet up in the next week or so. I'mma allow you two a little more time to cool off first. But just know, the three of us gotta eventually meet. A'ight?" Murder stated to her.

"Well, I'm down south again, Barry, and won't be able to meet up no time soon," Tati lied. She had no intentions to reconcile any of the differences she and Quana faced.

"Well, I'm sorry to be the one to inform you, but your ass is gonna have to cut that vacation short, baby girl. The shit we gotta fix, is far more important than that. And like I said, I'mma give you two hot bitches a week or so to cool off. So be prepared. No exceptions," Murder capped before he abruptly ended the call without so much as to allow Tati the opportunity to respond.

Murder knew the importance of fixing the relationship between the two. And if he failed to do so, all types of problems was subject to come his way. He wasn't about to let that happen on no accord. And especially not behind two females not being able to control their lustful desires they had over a dude who meant neither one of them any good.

Heeme was bad for business, no matter how it was to go at that point. But Tati and Quana failed to realize this! However, Murder didn't.

Chapter 11

The assassination of Ivan Ustinov went through smoothly for Herb. There wasn't a hitch of sloppiness in how he carried out the hit. Once Vladimir was able to confirm everything through the news media, another meeting between he and Herb was arranged. Herb made his way to Vladimir's car dealership located on Broad Street in North Philly. He had a good idea that the level of respectability from the Russians would now increase. The deed he'd done for them made it a mandatory thing that they look at him in a different way now.

Upon arrival, Herb was escorted by one of Vladimir's workers to the office space of the building. He was told to strip out of his clothing by Vladimir. "For security purposes," he was told. Herb didn't take it personal. The world he now played in required spur of the moment instances like that.

He had a thought.

It's gonna be many more days like this I'm sure, so long as I'm in bed with these type of people.

Vladimir spoke to Herb. "My friend. I'm gonna need for you to put on one of these," he instructed.

There were several gray colored Nike sweatsuits available to choose from. Sizes XL, 2XL, and 3XL. Vladimir had one on already. Apparently whatever the occasion was they were intent on being a part of, it required this style of dress.

"We must got somewhere else to go?" Herb had asked.

"Absolutely. Due to you doing the job so well and me speaking highly for you, someone who's further up our food chain wants to meet you for himself. We'll discuss business as we move forward. There's a possibility it may be more of these in the pipeline of this nature," Vladimir stated, agitating his trigger-finger to indicate *kill*.

"Well, I'm glad to know that my career in these vicious streets, is finally looking up to something. Things are paying off," Herb responded.

Once outfitted, Vladimir and Herb exited the office and got into Vladimir's black Audi A8. They headed to Center City Philadelphia. The destination was to one of the ritziest hotels the city had to offer, the Ritz-Carlton. Vladimir had a family member in town visiting. It was his uncle Vatale Bout, his father's second eldest brother. Vatale was next in line to lead the Bout clan. Vladimir's father suffered from a terminal illness and didn't have long to live. Someone would succeed him.

"Vlad, I've been in Philly my whole life, and haven't so much as tapped a toe inside a place this nice," Herb said upon their arrival at the hotel.

"Well . . . you're about to now, Herbie. A very important person wants to meet us. This is his favorite place to stay when in Philly," Vladimir responded.

They made a pit stop at the front desk. Security was focused on them intensely to begin with. But at the point of the visitors producing proper ID, the speculation and suspicion lessened and they were allowed permission to pass.

Vladimir led the way to the gym room of the hotel. The uncle loved to unwind with a light workout in the A.M. hours. The time was 9:00 that morning.

"So this the reason for the sweatsuits, I see," Herb remarked.

"Correct. This is exactly why. My uncle is into health and fitness," Vladimir responded.

He pulled his phone out and made a call. The person on the opposite end answered. The two began to speak in Russian.

"We're here," Vladimir said. "Only a few feet away."

"Okay," the uncle replied. "I'm in the sauna."

The call ended.

"It's about to get hot, Herbie."

"Oh, really. Why is that?"

"He's in the steam room."

The two entered and took notice of the uncle. He was seated in his under briefs without a shirt and a towel around his neck. He had a Bluetooth earpiece in and chatted with his assistant who was across from him. A space for two was reserved for Vladimir and Herb. Immediately, Vladimir and the uncle began to speak in Russian. Herb was introduced.

The uncle was a bit shocked to know it was a *black* guy the nephew trusted and relied upon to take care of the business of murder for them. Vladimir had never revealed this. Nonetheless, he held a high regard of Vladimir's judgment.

"Herbie. It's a pleasure to meet you," Vatale greeted, then extended his hand to shake his guest's.

"It's a pleasure to meet you as well, sir," Herb responded with grace.

"My nephew speaks highly of you. In many ways. But the one I'm most fond of, is the job that got rid of that ungrateful bastard Ivan."

"I thank you and your nephew for the opportunity to work my way up the ladder of success."

"My reasons for having you here today was to personally lay eyes upon you and to also give my blessing to Vladimir, to treat you well with some type of gift. That was a huge risk asked of you, and I feel the need to ensure you're rewarded well."

"Again, my pleasure. And there was no way I was gonna pass up the opportunity Vladimir offered. We've known one another for far too long and have been business acquaintances throughout at the same time," Herb said. His words were carefully chosen.

Vatale smiled at him. He was impressed with how Herb presented himself.

"Is there anything the Bout family may provide you as a bonus to further accommodate you? The Ivan job proved to be an outstanding deed you've done. And we'd like to show a deeper depth of gratitude towards you. If you'll accept?" Vatale stated.

"As a matter of fact . . . there may be. I have two requests to make, actually. The first, I'd like an increase in product, as I'm now a part of the network."

"Granted. I was looking to do so anyway," Vatale said.

"And the other request of mine, me and Vladimir can make this happen back at the dealership when we return. I saw a car I liked. It's nice too," Herb responded. He was sure to take advantage of each offer presented to him. This was the chance of a lifetime. He thought, *Damn! I'm making some serious moves for myself. A nigga got strong ties with the fuckin' Russian Mafia! Now how dope is this!*

Herb shed a tear. The other three took notice, even though he had sweat beads dotted about his head. Nonetheless, the emotion was apparent.

"What brings tears to your eyes, Herbie?" Vatale asked of him.

The Russians demonstrated a strong sense of order. No one spoke out of turn. And when Vatale spoke, the other two remained silent.

"I'm just in awe of it all, Mister Vatale." Vladimir had mentioned the name of the uncle to Herb while in the car on the way to the hotel. "That's all. I've worked hard and have patiently waited for the chance to prove myself. I've always wanted to establish my own hustle and do things the way I see fit. I mean, ever since I was a corner boy doing my thing, I always had to put in the work for someone else. But now, thanks to you all here, I'm able to reap the fruit of my own labor. And that's a good thing. A very good thing." Herb expressed his honest feelings while praising his Russian counterparts for inviting him in as a business partner.

"Your story sounds interesting, Herbie. I admire your ambition. But by the way, I never asked of you your actual name?" asked the uncle.

"My full name is Herbert Glover Jr., after my father," Herb replied. He pulled his driver's license from the wallet clip he had and politely handed it to the man hosting their meeting.

Vatale bowed his head in approval of Herb's true identity. His intention was to continue further in business with the new associate of theirs. "Vladimir, be sure to give him what he asks from you," the uncle said.

The pow-wow lasted all but twenty minutes. Vladimir and Herb then left the hotel and headed back to the dealership. During the ride back, the two friends began a conversation.

"Herbie. What was it you seen that captured your attention?" Vladimir asked. They were now pulling into the driveway of the dealership.

"That motherfucka' right there, bro!" Herb let out. He pointed in the direction of the car he was approaching. It was a gray colored, fully loaded, Mercedes Benz coupe. A new model.

This particular car had extraordinary features about it. The one to stand out to Herb was the gull wing doors that the vehicle had. He'd fallen in love with the car at first sight. He felt he had to have it.

I can see me and Imani in this car right now, riding shotgun, on our way to some important place. Or to some place where we can really enjoy ourselves, he thought, as he marveled at the vehicle.

"Oh. That one. Yeah. I liked that one myself. It's a nice car," Vladimir responded.

"Well, you did once like it. But it's mine now. And I'm so ready to drive it," Herb said in good nature.

"That one is gonna cost you a grip, bro. Because I like it too," Vladimir said with a smile.

"Come on Herbie, let's go inside, so we can get this paperwork situated, then you can be on your way."

They walked towards the office and entered. Once all the paperwork was processed and ownership of the car now belonged to Herb, he became eager as ever to get behind the wheel of the futuristic luxury mobile. He wanted to head home, get clean, and make the drive to D.C. on a surprise visit upon Imani. That became the plan for the day.

"Yo, bro, keep the Beamer here for me and give it a full tune up, ok? I'll be back in a few days to pick it up," Herb said to Vladimir.

Vladimir handed him the keys.

"Herbie, I fixed the documents to look like you paid twenty grand in deposit and will lease it at a thousand a month. This probably the most expensive gift you've ever received, huh?"

"It is! Ivan proved to be a lottery ticket for me. I went from poverty to riches, from a Beamer to a dope Benz!" Herb humored.

Vladimir seemed to always be mesmerized at the street philosophy Herb used. He had a stylistic way of phrasing things.

Vroom! Vroom! Vroom! Herb revved the engine a few times once he started the car. He and Vladimir exchanged a few more words as Herb took a seat inside and allowed the doors to the car to remain open. Vladimir handed him the paperwork to the car and he immediately pulled out his phone to make a call. He contacted his insurance company. He began speaking with them while exiting the lot on the way to their office.

Once all of his business was handled at the insurance office, Herb went home. He pulled from his closet a nice casual set of clothing. There were a pair of slacks, a button-down shirt, and a pair of expensive shoes by Bally to match. His carry-all bag was already packed with personal essentials to take him through the weekend. The last time he and Imani came together, she took a trip to Philly. It was now his turn to visit her in D.C.. There was reason to celebrate, he felt. He'd elevated a notch in the line of business he was in. The day was a Thursday, and Herb felt the need not to return until that Sunday night or either Monday morning, depending.

Herb showered, dressed, then exited the house and getting into the Benz. He hit I-95 on the road to the "Chocolate City." He ate sunflower seeds and drank apple juice along the way. A phone call was made to Imani to notify her that he was in traffic as they spoke, and on his way to her for the weekend. Imani became excited at the thought. She was falling madly in love with Herb. The two stayed on one another's mind. It was as if they were made for one another.

PART TWO

Chapter 12

Hours Later...

Herb pulled into the city limits of the nation's capital. He checked into the Marriott Hotel as he wanted to rest up briefly before the weekend fun with Imani was to begin. The long drive had him tired in a way.

At 6:30 P.M., he'd awakened and began to prep for the night. His phone vibrated. He had an incoming call. It was from someone he hadn't spoken to in weeks. A lot had taken place throughout the time, and a need was there for them to update one another on the progress they'd made. It was the homie Murder on the opposite end of the line.

"Bro. What's been good with you!" Herb had answered. "Ain't heard a squeak outta you in a minute, my nigga. What's the deal?"

"Shit, bro. A nigga just been trying to maintain in these vicious streets. What about you?" Murder asked. *"These Vicious Streets,"* had become a catch phrase that had slithered into the vernacular of the streets all throughout Philly. It was used heavily by Murder and Herb.

"You say you trying to maintain. Shit, I have been maintaining, bro. Everything with my Russian *boul* Vlad, been panning out like I knew it would. Got blessed with a luxury gift and the whole nine, yo."

"Oh, yeah? A luxury gift? Like what?"

"Nothing too special. A little whip, that's all. A Benz coupe with gull wings on it, like it's about to fly away when

87

I open both doors," Herb made mention of it in an excited way. "It's a rare type of car for a street nigga in Philly."

"That's dope. I can't wait to see what it looks like. And I'm assuming that the pipeline with Vlad bearing fruit. Things been well on my end too. Opposite the bullshit my sister and our cousin Tatiana got going on over a piece of dick. And speaking of that. I don't know how, but I found out that Quana's boyfriend, so happened to have had a few bricks of the work that was stolen from us."

"Get the fuck outta here! How did that happen?" Herb asked.

Murder then gave him the rundown over everything but left out the part about the work and the money that was taken back from Heeme. He thought maybe Herb may ask for half of it, and he'd already given every penny of it to Charlotte. Also, Murder was still conducting his own investigation into the situation. So, there wasn't a necessity to let Herb know all the details. Not to mention the fact that Herb was now making serious moves in a different market with another product. He didn't care to deal in heroin any longer.

"What's up with you and Imani, bro?"

"I can't have it any better than I do with her, bro. Actually, I'm in D.C. now. I'mma be here for the weekend," Herb responded.

"Oh word? I'm in D.C. myself. Been parlaying at Charlotte's spot lately. We making serious progress. We've been contemplating buying a crib together in Philly," Murder revealed.

"Oh, for real? That is real progress. But what you plan to do with your young jawn, Brooklyn? Not to bring up the fact you mentioned you and your Puerto Rican sweetheart reconnecting after many years of being apart. How you gonna balance all that?"

"Shit, nigga. You know me. I'll figure something out," Murder replied. He gave a quick, ready-made answer.

"Nigga, please! That's a lot to figure out! Three different females with three different situations, and they all high maintenance! *Sheeez*, my nigga! But I'm sure you'll get it right."

"I really ain't got no choice. If I'm tryna hold on to all three of 'em like I plan to, I have good reasons to. But anyway, you tryna link up this weekend? You and Imani with me and Charlotte?"

"That sounds like a plan. We can do that. I'm sure they'll be down to double date," Herb responded.

"That's a bet, bro. Just let 'Mani know what the lick read and we'll see you two tomorrow or Saturday."

"No doubt, my nigga. One!" Herb lastly stated.

"One!" Murder replied then ended the call.

Herb got dressed once more then made his way to Imani's house. He was eager to see her.

***

Upon arrival, he hopped out the car leaving the door open, and swaggered to the front door. She was already opening it for him by the time he reached. Imani was excited as ever to see him again, and the car he now drove enhanced her perception for him. Herb brought along a few gifts for her as well.

She stood and looked on at him as he approached. Her full head of hair was blown out in a bushy Afro style. She were putting in a set of earrings to match her outfit. Imani had features like that of the star tennis player Naomi Osaka, from the hair down to the rounded bedroom eyes she was in possession of. There was a heightened sensation and appeal about the brown skin cutie.

"What you think, sweetie?" Herb asked.

"That's a nice ride you have there, baby. I can't wait to get behind the wheel of it," she expressed.

"You may get the chance to do that this evening," Herb responded. He was now face-to-face with her.

They kissed. She loved it when his romantic side was being shown. This was adored by her. A man and his sensibilities.

"You didn't have a hard time getting here, did you?" she asked, referring more to his travel on the interstate than the GPS leading him to her doorstep.

"Nah. Everything was smooth sailing," Herb responded. He was now inside the house.

He took a look around in observance of the oriental decor and influence the living room display.

"You're from Asian ancestry?" he asked.

"Yes sir, I am. My grandmother. She was from South Korea. My grandparents met during the time of the Korean War. My grandfather was in the military. He was born and raised in Virginia. He had tremendous ambition and a strong will. When the war ended, he brought my grandmother to America," Imani made him aware.

"Oh wow! That explains the hair, the skin complexion, the eyes, and your features. You're a very gorgeous woman, Imani."

Herb poured on the compliments. He was a charming dude.

"You must be trying to really sweet me off my feet and us get married or something? Because you're not about to be filling my head up with all these sentimental words of affection and have me wanting to be all close to you every day, and we're not fully committed to one another. At least not yet," Imani let out.

They kissed once more.

"Who knows. I just may be ready to offer you something, at least. To let you know I'm for real about you."

"Oh, you are? And what's that?"

Herb went low to his socks and brought out a sapphire birthstone ring. It had a rose gold band to it.

"I got this for you, Imani. A promise ring."

Herb then went into the other sock.

"And these," he acknowledged, and produced a pair of heart shaped earrings. They were rose gold as well. "I take notice of your face each time Charlotte brags to you about all that Barry has bought for her. So, I felt the need to make you feel special and appreciated too," Herb said with a smile.

Imani began to cry behind his kind words and gestures. He was going above and beyond to please her. His part was being played well.

"Herb, you're gonna mess around and have me fall so in love with you. And there's no telling how deep my love can go."

They tongue kissed there in the moment. Imani then led the way to her bedroom so she could continue to get dressed for the night.

"And speaking of Barry and Charlotte, he's here in D.C. too, and they both thought it a good idea to double date tomorrow or Saturday. If you're ok with that?" Herb brought it to her attention.

"No problem. We can do so. That way, I'll have a chance to flaunt my ring now," Imani stated, as she held out her hand and looked on at the lovely gift Herb provided.

Shortly thereafter, they'd left her house and were en route to enjoy an elegant meal at a Korean eatery. Imani had a taste for this. The night was still young and the two then went to a nice lounge that offered great cocktails and a line of neo-soul singers who visited often. Once they'd had a fair share of drinks and pleasant music, they made their way to Herb's hotel suite to cap off the occasion. The intention was to provide the best sex that either of the two may have ever had.

Between rounds of sex, Imani brought up the idea to Herb of her moving to Philly. Surprisingly, Herb wanted nothing more than for the transition to occur for them both. He approved for it to happen sooner rather than later. And that there wasn't a need for her to wait on Charlotte to do so first.

Herb wanted Imani there long before the friend was to relocate. In the next weeks to come, their plan was to go out in and around Philly to hunt for a home.

Overall, Herb's weekend in D.C. was set to go very well. They did double date, fucked more like crazy, and discussed business plans that they could initiate together. They were on a path to do well and succeed as a couple.

Chapter 13

Weeks Later . . .

Ever since the stabbing attack Highway suffered, chaos followed from within his own crew. Nothing seemed to go correctly. Treachery prevailed. Money from the sale of the product wasn't checked in, and Ruiz applied pressure about being paid. Atop it all, Highway was paralyzed from the neck down. His disability prevented him from being in the mix of things putting in the work to correct the wrongs. Damage was done to his nerves and spine. The predicament he was in made him an invalid. To make matters worse, his memory was altered and speech impacted, and he was the only soul who knew where those two hundred and-thirty remaining kilos of heroin were located. Not to mention the fact that he couldn't speak either so to tell someone to secure them. All he was able to do was rotate his eyes and blink here and there. Nothing more. It appeared to be a done deal for Highway. The world he once knew was no more. The life changing attack messed him up for real. And with this, it may complicate things for the feds who was investigating him, and on the agreement that was in place for Ralphie Arroyo.

The brother, Uriel, attempted to gain command of the crews, but it was too late. There wasn't much he could do. Too much trouble ran rampant throughout the ranks of the PRDs, and there wasn't any product to make money from to fix things. Uriel began to demand answers. The security men who was supposed to have protected Highway that night, had a lot of explaining to do. That included Ralphie. But by the time he could be told to meet with the new leader, he was long gone and nowhere to be found.

Why run if you have nothing to hide? thought Uriel over the strange behavior of Ralphie. *Maybe he helped set my brother up to be hit.*

The conspiracy theories began to run wild in Uriel's mind. And not only that. He and Highway had the problem approaching to deal with regarding Ruiz possibly sending his hit squad to wipe them out behind not being paid the money he was owed. At the time when Highway was last supplied, he did mention to his brother how much product he'd received and the money that had to go to Ruiz. But they had never anticipated the traumatic events that befallen upon them with the attack.

For some reason, Highway had developed a level of arrogance and a heightened sense of invincibility about himself. In his mind before the attack, he thought he couldn't be touched, being that he was one of the top narcotic kingpins in Philly. But then, it happened. And a man who was once so high up, now held a different position down low at the very bottom.

Dark Skinned Jermaine, utilized the information he was fed from the street to put his moves in place. He knew who was connected to who along the network, and one by one, he was looking to knock them out of his path on his way to be seated upon the throne of the Philly underworld. His exit from prison was to be an epic occasion.

Team Highway and the PRDs had problems to deal with on three different fronts; one with Ruiz; one with the feds behind Ralphie snitching to them; and one with the hitter who was on the loose who could strike again at any moment's notice. Uriel didn't know what to do.

***

Jabari managed to make all the necessary moves and passed the requirement to make the transition from uniform officer to the robbery/homicide division as a detective. He adapted to his new position well. The district he was assigned to work cases was in West Philly. There had been a string of killings throughout the city between rival gangs and street crews. War was waged with retaliations happening around the clock. Mostly over territory and narcotics deals going afoul. The streets was on fire, and Jabari and the supervisor he was under, Detective Arnold Specter, had work cut out for them.

While in the office one day, Jabari and his investigative colleagues were getting a tongue lashing like no other during briefing. Their superior gave them hell over two separate slayings they needed to have resolved. The first was over an entrepreneurial minded and philanthropic pillar of Philadelphia. He was a political aspirant named Errol Lawler, who was murdered in his own home in the wee hours one morning. And the second, was the most disturbing of them both. The brutal murder of a pregnant female by the name of Shavika Felton. She'd been bludgeoned to death with a bat by her assailant. The police commissioner didn't care whether or not these crimes occurred in the respective districts that the detectives were assigned. He ordered everyone to disregard boundary lines and come together to find out who killed these specific people and make significant arrests. The police department was receiving negative publicity over the fact of not being able to effectively solve homicides. The great upstanding citizens of Philly were upset with law enforcement, and something needed to be done.

To make matters worse for the police commissioner, the pregnant female was the great niece of the mayor, and he called almost daily wanting results. Also, the governor of the state, a Philly native himself, chimed in on the elevated violent crime rate of the city. The department had an entire ocean of hot water to work their way out of as City Hall, the place where Shavika worked, cut them no slack. There was a need to save face by the department and do all necessary to regain the trust of the public, which they served and protected.

With no potential suspects nor any evidence to point them in the right direction, the police didn't know where to start. However, there were a couple of witnesses to call in and reported seeing a UPS truck make a delivery at the home of the pregnant female. There were not one but two persons that appeared. The investigators recovered a large freight package inside the victim's home that hadn't been ordered online and had no tracking number on it. The baby crib was purchased at Walmart. The homicide detectives now had something to work with to help narrow the investigation. Also, the GPS of the UPS truck revealed that indeed, a stop was made at the home of the victim along the daily commute. The driver who was assigned the truck could be the possible killer, the detectives assumed, and an arrest for questioning was now needed.

Philly homicide contacted UPS and was provided the name of the driver who purportedly had driven the truck that day. A guy named LaShawn Norton. GPS data also proved that the truck was parked at Felton's residence for at least fifteen minutes. The issue was that there wasn't supposed to have been a delivery at the specific address. At no time. Norton had a lot of explaining to do. And while in custody, he spewed all he knew. Even though they had an airtight alibi to exclude him as being the actual killer, that didn't eliminate him from being an accomplice or an accessory to the crime.

Throughout the interrogation, the police only provided little information to Norton on all they knew about the Felton killing. The hope was to catch him up in lies, then eventually pin the murder on him to solve the case. However, his story was the truth, and he wanted to free himself of the ordeal they put him through at all cost. Norton provided a name of a female he had carried on a sexual affair with. A Tatiana Fredricks. The focus was now placed upon identifying and finding her, and Norton was held until further notice.

Although Jabari didn't have a direct hand in on the Felton slaying investigation, he had a colleague who did. The two maintained a decent rapport, and Jabari was made aware of all they had regarding the case and who they were looking for at the moment. He immediately knew who Tatiana Fredricks was, and now needed to talk with his brother to know his side of the story.

Once off from work for the day, Jabari immediately contacted Murder. They definitely needed to talk. In person. The meeting place was at Penn's Landing. Jabari called Murder while he was on his way to the meeting spot.

"Yeah, what's good, Bari! How you, bro?" Murder answered.

"Nigga, we got problems brewing! And it ain't looking good!" Jabari stated in an emphatic tone of voice.

"What the fuck! What you mean by that, bro?"

"The thing I'm trying to find out is, how the fuck you get so sloppy? The thing with Mage? The chick?" Jabari said.

"Look, say less. I'm on my way to Penn's Landing right now as we speak. Get there ASAP!"

The call was ended.

Nearly thirty minutes later, Murder was at the location talking with Jabari

"How were you so sloppy, Barry? That shit on the verge of getting outta hand now."

"Bro, that job was done proper. I would want to believe," Murder said to defend himself. "We haven't had any backlash so far."

"No the fuck that job wasn't proper! It was extra sloppy! Now who the fuck you had to do the work for you? And don't lie to me either, nigga! I already know all I'm supposed to know," stated Jabari.

Murder knew he had to be truthful. A lie wouldn't work. He didn't know what all Jabari knew, and they had too much serious business going on for him not to keep it real. He spoke his truth.

"A'ight look, bro. I ain't gonna lie. I didn't do that one myself. But the other one on the dude, I did," he confessed.

"Look, bro! I'm only talking about the one specifically job concerning the female. That's it."

"Nah, bro. I couldn't do that one. My conscience wouldn't allow me to," Murder answered.

"Then why the fuck did you agree to do it, if you ain't have the gut to do it? All you did was fuck things up, nigga!" Jabari said vehemently. He gritted his teeth from anger.

"What the fuck happened, bro? How did I fuck up?"

"Nigga, you still haven't answered my question. Who-the-fuck did you put up to do it for you?"

"I had a female cousin of mine do it for me—"

"Tatiana Fredricks, right?" Jabari cut him off to say.

For a moment, Murder found himself having to think over his cousin's full name. He hadn't heard it in a long time.

"Yeah. Her. How the fuck you know that, bro?"

Jabari gave Murder a cold look behind him asking such a dumb ass question as he had, without realizing, that the elder brother was a cop. Eventually, Murder was able to read between the lines and comprehend the message conveyed in Jabari's body language.

"That's your uncle Kev's daughter, right?"

"Yeah, bro. That's her. But what the fuck they got on her?"

"Too much! Too fucking much! That's all I got to say on that. And the only way we're gonna be able to stop any further damage from being done and prevent all the other shit from being exposed we got going on is, she's gotta go! It's just that simple. And you're gonna be the one to get rid of her ass. It's your mess. You gotta clean it up. This is the only way to eliminate the threat of prosecution, by making Tatiana disappear. We can't afford for her to be arrested.

Because if she is, we're doomed! Everything they got already leads straight to her. And no more her, mean no more case. It'll all come to an end. Just that simple. Now I've said all I need to say on that. And no, I didn't mention anything to Mage. So don't worry. Just cancel that bitch Tatiana. And that should do it," Jabari lastly stated.

He thumped the butt of what remained of the Black and Mild into the river, then casually walked away from Murder. Jabari didn't even allow Murder the opportunity to reply. His final words to his brother was law. Literally and figuratively. The same as his badge authorized him to be.

Chapter 14

Murder knew he had to hurry to have Tatiana meet up with him. That way, he could trap her, then finally knock her off as he'd been ordered to do. Little did he know, Tatiana was already alerted by LaShawn, that the police was looking for her to question about the Shavika Felton murder. LaShawn left out a lot that he'd learned during his interrogation. He lied to the police, by telling them that while he was asleep inside the motel, Tatiana stole the truck from him, and that's how it was taken from his possession.

The story LaShawn provided corroborated the surveillance from the motel where he'd reserved in his own name. And the cops wasn't able to charge him because there was no evidence that implicated him no type of way. They had no choice but to turn him loose.

Damn! That stupid bitch fucked up bad and made me fuck up at the same time. Now I gotta be the one to take her out to save us. But fuck it! It is what it is at this point. I gotta do what I gotta do, Murder thought.

He pulled out his phone to call Tati. Her number was no longer in service.

"What the fuck!" he spat.

He attempted once more to be sure he wasn't tripping. Same results. He had no way to get in touch with her now.

Tati had gotten smart about the situation. She made it her business to go to her mother's house to lay low. No one on her father's side of the family had any idea where the mother

THESE VICIOUS STREETS 3 | PRINCE A. TAUHID

lived. Atop of that, Tati altered her appearance to help her hide from others knowing who she was. The police had no record of her, no photos, and neither did LaShawn. All they knew was she had a biracial background, but no face to match. She'd switched up and fully embraced her Puerto Rican roots. She knew the Spanish language fluently and could easily fake like she didn't speak English if it came to it. But no matter what the situation now appeared to be, her determination was to stay out the way and continue to make progress with Heeme. There was no way she was going to allow what they had to go in vain. Their lives were nearly taken to be together. Also they too began to plot in their own way and had plans to get Murder and Quana. The beef was about to intensify.

***

Bright and early the next day, a Wednesday, Murder got up and contacted Quana. He needed her to hit the road to return to Philly so they could talk in person, and she could let him know all he wanted her to tell him about the hit she and Tati did on the Felton female.

"Yeah. What's up, bro?" Quana answered.

She sounded as if she was beat down about it all. Like she had no idea on what to do moving forward. Basically, the girl was lovesick and hurt behind Heeme.

"Good morning," Murder greeted.

"Good morning, bro."

"Everything good on y'all end? Mommy getting her act together?"

He spoke in a mild polite tone for a change, not wanting to make matters worse by communicating aggressively.

"Everything good, bro. Mommy's sobering up at a steady pace. She was dope sick here and there. But Randle helped her make it through those phases. She told me to tell you that she's sorry too. It sounded like she really meant it. And I'm at a hotel. I wanted to give them some private time and I needed some myself," Quana related.

"We've heard that outta Mommy before. But so long as she's good. And I need you to hit the road today and come home. I got some deep shit I need to speak with you in person about. I can't over the phone."

"That Tati shit again?"

"Not just *that Tati shit* by itself. That *you and Tati shit* this time. A mess has been made. And we gotta clean it up."

"Damn! I know you not able to rest easy these days, are you?"

"And the media hasn't either. Come to find out, the jawn was related to some pretty big people here in the city. But we're gonna get into all that when you get here."

"So what about the Heeme situation? You think it's safe now?" Quana asked.

"Quana, the way you told me how you got at that nigga and Tati, I'm more than sure he don't want no smoke. And besides, I'm at my penthouse in Center City. Also, you can park your car and get around in my low-key ride. Or I can have Brooklyn swap with you and you can drive her whip while she takes yours to New York."

"I think I like that idea better. The Brooklyn one. She's got New York plates, right?"

"Yep. And you can lay low here at my main spot until me and my dudes track that nigga down and put his ass away."

"So I finally get a chance to kick it in the penthouse how I want to, huh?"

"I would've been let you do that. But you were too close to that snake-ass nigga you had in your life. And I was scared you may do too much talking around him. Besides, you already got a lot of explaining to do. And you know exactly what I'm talking about. That money and work I got outta your closet."

"Bro, I had nothing to do with that. On God, I didn't. I can't even begin to tell you how Heeme ended up with something that belonged to you."

"That's easy for you to say. But it might be harder for you to convince me otherwise. We're gonna talk about it though. This afternoon in fact. You just get your ass on up here in the next few hours, a'ight?" Murder demanded.

"No doubt, bro. I'll be there," Quana said lastly.

The two siblings concluded the call.

Quana knew for sure it had to be something really urgent for her brother to call her in the A.M. like that and instruct her to come home in the midst of all the tension between them and the enemy. And also, Quana began to question herself on how exactly Heeme just so happened to have gotten his hands on a product that belonged to Murder. The situation was crazy on all ends, and they now had the duty to come up with a resolutions to move forward.

***

Hours Later . . .

Quana was now back in Philly like she was told to be. The first and only stop she made was to Murder's penthouse suite. He was already anticipating her arrival by the time she'd made it there, and had company with him too, being the two was intent on going out to put in some serious work to rid themselves of the threat.

Murder hated the feeling of being on edge and in a paranoid state. The reality of the situation was a call to action, for him, and his number one hitter, Traino.

Once inside and situated in the living room, the conversation began.

"So, what's good, bro? I'm here. Talk to me," Quana said. She was seated comfortably on the couch.

"First things first. The more important shit. Give me the rundown on everything Tati mentioned to you about the female y'all did?"

Quana immediately explained what she'd been told and how Tati convinced her to get involved. The only thing she didn't say was who actually did the killing.

"So which one of y'all killed her?" he asked bluntly.

"Come on, bro! The street name of my one and only sibling is Murder! How the fuck you couldn't figure out, that the apple didn't fall far from the tree! You know I had to be the one to do that shit, nigga! That punk-bitch Tati, ain't got that type of energy in her heart to put in that kind of work, Quana gave an honest confession. She continued. "But, bro, what I'm tryna know is, why you just didn't just come to me to begin with, for me to have handled that for you?"

"It's because . . . you're my sister, and I didn't want you to have nothing to do with that no type of way."

"Well guess what? That same shit you tried so hard to avoid, I ended up a part of anyway. And, the one to do all the work. So how far did you get with all that being careful shit? Nowhere fast, and in a whole lot of other drama to deal with behind it," Quana stated.

"Shit, truth be, it really ain't no never mind why I didn't approach you first about it anyway. What's done is done. We can't do nothing but move on and eliminate the main piece to it all at this point."

"Tell us what you can about this nigga, Heeme?" Traino said, breaking his silence. He and Quana were already familiar with one another through the long-time friendship between he and Murder.

She related as much about the now ex-boyfriend as she could, along with how he could be located and all else. Murder found the information useful.

So Quana, I'm more than sure I don't have to explain the direction we about to go now, do I? The three of us here?" Murder asked.

"Give it to me straight, bro, so it won't be any misunderstanding on my part," Quana responded.

She was sure to ask the right question this time. Enough fuck ups had already occurred, and they didn't need anymore.

"It's really simple, Quana. Find the people we looking for, hit 'em properly, then get away. And be sure we do a good enough job while we at it. The both of them gotta get it!" Murder spat emphatically.

"Damn! Tati too?" Quana let out. "She's gotta go?"

"Yep! That bitch too! She's gotta go!" Murder retorted. "And you're gonna be the one to do her. Since you already done inherited all this mess y'all created behind a dick!"

"Damn, Tati. why the fuck you couldn't just leave my man alone and find you one for yourself? It wouldn't have had to come to this," Quana stated under her breath.

"It's too late to say a prayer for that bitch now! I've already been ordered to do so. Traino gonna take care of Heeme. And you and me gonna trap Tati, for you to cancel her party."

Murder made the plan clearly known.

Quana looked from Murder to Traino then back to Murder again. Although the two hitters had a grin of delight about their faces, Quana knew that neither of them niggaz was bullshitting. They had no time to play.

With Traino aka "Trained To Go" being the more dangerous of the duo, he was eager for action. Especially so against any family members of those JBM niggaz whom he felt betrayed he and his family. Reason being, the youngster who was executed on the order of the JBM leader at the time (Aaron Jones) inside a grocery store out in West Philly, happened to have been the half-brother of Traino. They had the same father. This happened to also be the same incident which landed Aaron on Pennsylvania's death row in the early nineties.

Traino's family still had vengeance in their hearts and blood in their eyes. But to avoid yet another clash of the titans, a truce was agreed upon. However, now that the nephew of Aaron's—*Heeme*—had fucked up and sparked a new war between a different generation, he'd made himself fair game, and Traino was looking to pull his card. It was on and popping.

Chapter 15

One Week Later . . .

Charlotte contacted Murder to make him aware that she and Ni'Asia wanted to travel to Philly for the weekend to spend time with him and for them to begin looking for a home. She also was looking to hang out with Lori, so that they may become better acquainted and know the ways of the other. He was still there in Philly, conducting business and didn't see why not allow his lady and her daughter the opportunity. Murder wanted more quality time anyway, and this was ideal for the both of them.

For some reason, Murder had a tendency to underestimate the capabilities of Heeme. He was a street dude himself and took all beef as a drastic threat to his life. This was something to concern himself with.

Murder felt that his reputation in the streets alone, was enough to keep Heeme at bay until he and Traino had the drop on him to kill. But there was no fear on Heeme's behalf, as he felt that if a well thought out hit on Murder by him was to take place, that would earn him a big stain in the streets to be reckoned with, then he'd have the juice. Not Murder any longer. However, for the particular weekend at hand, Murder had the duty to keep his girl and her daughter safe under his watch and enjoy the time they were to share together.

Charlotte hit the highway at the very moment she picked up Ni'Asia from school. To her surprise, the daughter had a hot topic on her mind she wanted to talk about. One that the mother hadn't thought would ever occur. The opportunity was ideal for the youngster as she'd had a short day at school, it was the beginning of the weekend, and she knew her mother loved to talk anytime they travel.

"Mom, can I ask you something, please?" Ni'Asia requested.

"Sure, baby. Go ahead, what's on your mind?"

"What I wanted to ask you was . . . when will I have the chance to be with my dad again? I miss him," the little girl said.

Charlotte was at a complete loss for words. She was completely taken aback and held spellbound by the question. There was a need for her to think up something quick to say in response.

"When will you have a chance to be with your dad again?" Charlotte retorted. "You asked as if you have a memory of him or something, baby."

"That's because I do. I remember him well," Ni'Asia made her mother aware. At the same time, a level of fear was finding its way back into Charlotte's life as it was during the time her and Reign Man was together.

"Oh! You do?"

"Umm-hmm! I remember his name and all," Ni'Asia said.

Charlotte, now startled by the revelation, felt the need to know more of what the daughter may had known or had heard through the years. For security purposes at least.

She looked on at Ni'Asia with her mouth wide and began to form her next questions to ask.

"Well, what was his name then?"

"His name was 'Rain Man,'" the little girl answered.

"Ni'Asia! How you remember that?" Charlotte asked. She appeared to be in a state of hysteria with her outburst.

Judging by the tone of her mother's voice, the little girl didn't know if she was being chastised or what. All she'd done was repeat a name. Her father used to repeat a name to her in bedtime stories he recited almost daily. Charlotte had no knowledge of the early connection the father and daughter established. She would normally be too busy in the den of their home or bedroom watching TV or talking on the phone. But on the opposite end of things, Charlotte held belief that maybe Ni'Asia had heard a lot and began researching names on the internet.

"Momma, what did I say wrong? What did I do to make you raise your voice at me?" Ni'Asia asked in fear.

"I'm sorry, baby. Mommy so sorry. I didn't mean to get loud with you. I was just curious to know how you remember so well as you do. That's all." Charlotte made a return to her normal senses.

"Daddy used to read and sing to me. I still remember the song he made with his name in it."

"And how did it go? Sing it for me, baby," Charlotte requested.

Ni'Asia smiled and began to be happy once more. She was asked to put her talents on display. Many kids loved these moments.

"Okay-okay. Daddy used to say, '*No one could stop the rain, my baby Ni'Asia's a queen. No one can stop the rain, Ni'Asia will rule as queen.*' That's what Daddy used to say. And every time it would rain, he would tell me not to be sad about it, because the rain mean a lot. We ate ice cream and other sweet stuff together on rainy days," she said.

Charlotte was shocked. She didn't know her own daughter as much as she thought. But, the truth of the matter was, Ni'Asia was blessed with the genetics and blood lineage she had. A hereditary rare condition was within her that caused keen memory in the youth at early ages beginning at nine months. The traits of the condition is found mostly in females of the Indigo children, and traces back many years. The Native American spiritualist elite demonstrated this most. Reign Man's family lay claims to this, as they're direct descendants thereof. His grandmother,

Iris Aikens was noted for having this condition. Her fore parents and ancestors prayed, chanted, and possessed an obsession for the rain. The same as Reign Man began teaching his daughter, in his own way, his grandmother had done the same for him and his sister.

Charlotte spoke more. "Baby, I can't say when you'll be able to spend time with your dad again, let alone, get to see him. He abandoned us. He wanted nothing to do with us, Ni'Asia. And that's why it's been you and me all this time. But Barry, he's been here for us. Don't you like him?"

Charlotte knew it was best to change the subject before being forced to answer more questions. Nonetheless, Ni'Asia was no fool and getting smarter by the day. Charlotte had plans to someday tell her daughter everything that they'd been through. The timing wasn't right at the moment. It was simply too soon.

***

Hours Later . . .

Charlotte and Ni'Asia were now pulling into the city limits of Philly. Murder had already texted her the address to the penthouse. Her GPS helped her get directly to his residence. The building was nice. Murder paid just over a million at five thousand monthly for the suite he owned. Of course after a hefty deposit was put down first. It was located in an affluent neighborhood downtown.

Barry never mentioned to me anything about him owning a goddamn penthouse! This place looks fabulous! Charlotte thought at the sight of the tower. She was in awe.

"Momma. Is Barry rich?" Ni'Asia asked.

"I have no idea right now, baby. None," she responded.

Charlotte then had a look back at the address to be sure everything was correct. It was. She hit Google Search for the map to appear. The locator on her phone pinpointed her at the address site. The images to appear on the search engine were of the building they stood in front of.

"Apparently, Barry must do have money, for him to be living this good," Charlotte said under her breath to herself.

She texted him.

CHARLOTTE: Barry, me and Ni'Asia are here in front of this beautiful building you live in. Why you never told me you lived so well? Lol!

He immediately responded.

BARRY: Lol! I was gonna tell you. I just had to get to know you first before revealing more of my personal self. I'm private like that in many ways. I'm on the way down to meet you two now.

He took the elevator to the lobby.

"Hello-hello-hello! Welcome! This is where I live. The Rittenhouse Condominium Plaza," he greeted with a smile on his face.

He and Charlotte kissed. He knelled and pecked Ni'Asia on the forehead. Murder reminisced over the times he would show the same affection to his very own daughter as he had Ni'Asia. He was a devastated man during the grieving process. But at the same time, Murder failed to realize that the hurt he felt at the loss of his daughter, was what the family felt of the people he'd killed. If not more. His loss wasn't equal to the ten or more taken at his hands. The acts to earn him the nickname, "Murder Murdoch."

Charlotte marveled in thought of her and Murder having it going on as a couple. *If only I could get Barry to clean up his act and go completely legit.* "Barry, this place is beautiful," Charlotte let out.

"You ain't seen nothing yet, just wait until you have a view of the city from the balcony of my suite," he responded. He lived on the fortieth floor. The building had forty-eight in total.

The bellhop walked over to help with their bags. They all were a complement for the residence of the building, courtesy of the Berk-Hath conglomerates who owned it.

Murder, Charlotte, and Ni'Asia made it to his penthouse. Once inside, his guests had the opportunity to observe the luxurious accommodations that the bachelor's haven had there. Dude loved the pool table that was set up in the entertainment section.

"This is where I rest my head most nights," he said to them.

"I'm ready to see that view over the city you bragged about," Charlotte stated. She smiled in an ecstatic fashion.

"Me too, Mommy," Ni'Asia chimed into say.

"Come on. Follow me," Murder said.

The three made steps towards the sliding glass door. Murder had a luxury set of tables and chairs to accentuate the platform.

"We're gonna sit out here and chill tonight," he made them aware of what the plan was.

Murder's cell phone vibrated on his hip. He had an incoming call from a person he hadn't talked to in a few weeks. It was Felicia. She wanted to see him again and possibly set up a date for them. He left Charlotte and Ni'Asia on the balcony and went to his bedroom to talk briefly. He let Felicia know that he'd be by shortly but couldn't stay too long. Family was in town, and he had to attend to the guest respectfully.

Charlotte and Ni'Asia were tired from the ride and wanted to rest up. It was still early in the day, just after 3:00 P.M. While they were to nap, this would be the opportunity Murder could use to go and meet with his Puerto Rican sensation. Then upon return, he could treat his girlfriend and her daughter to a shopping spree down on one of the most popular districts in all of Philly, South Street.

He left the penthouse, got into one of his low-profile vehicles and headed towards the nursing center where

Felicia told him to meet her. She was there to check up on her father.

Nearly twenty minutes later he was there, in the northeast section of the city. Felicia awaited him in the lobby.

"Hello, Barry! I'm glad to see you again. I'm happy you have the time to spend with me," she greeted him.

The two then hugged and kissed.

"I'm glad to see you as well, Felicia. I missed you, sweetheart," Murder responded.

They walked out the facility and got into his car for a ride and heavy conversation. He had a lot on his mind he wanted to talk about and so did she. It seemed to have been a long time coming. One that was worth the wait.

Chapter 16

Two Hours Later . . .

Murder was still out and about. Charlotte and Ni'Asia awakened from their nap. Once done taking a shower and dressing again, they took a seat in the living room to watch a TV show. Ni'Asia wasn't the type to sit anytime she was excited about something. So she got to her feet and made her way back to the balcony to view the city once more. Charlotte had something on her mind. A particular person to be exact. She needed to be updated on something.

In that instance, she grabbed her phone and scrolled through the contacts to get to her mother's information. She called.

"Hello!" answered Ms. Linda.

"Hey, Momma. How you been?"

"Carmen. Hey. I've been well. Didn't think you were going to call back anytime soon. But I see I was wrong. I miss you, baby. You and my granddaughter."

"I'm sure you do, Momma," Charlotte responded in a somber tone." You'll be able to see us again soon. I promise."

"I'm hoping so. Because I can't continue to go on this way."

"I really wish it wasn't like this, Momma. But it is. Did you ever reach out to Shug for me?"

"I did."

"And?"

"She agreed to talk. But only because it was me doing the begging for you."

"Begging! Momma!" Charlotte retorted.

"That girl despises you now, Carmen. For whatever her reasons may be," her mother made her aware. "And I'm not one of them, but you put a lot of people on your bad side."

"I'm understanding that. But don't nobody know the half of what I had to go through in my life with Vershon. That man did me so wrong. And everybody wants to blame me for simply saving me and my daughter from the destruction he caused. That bastard!" Charlotte vented.

"Let's not get all upset, baby. Okay. If nobody else feels your pain, Momma do. And no matter what, I'm on your side," the mother confirmed.

Her love for Charlotte was without an ending.

"I know you are, Momma. And I love you."

"Momma love you too. Now, take down this number so you can call your friend and you two talk. And you be sure to call me back once the both of you are done. Okay."

"Yes ma'am, Momma. I will."

Ms. Linda provided Charlotte with Shug's number. She wasted no time to initiate contact. A text was sent through a communications app. One she had a second phone number established on.

CHARLOTTE: Shug it's me. Blossom.

The two previously declared themselves the *black* version of Blossom and Six during the heydays the show aired. They loved it.

A reply came through shortly thereafter.

SHUG: I hope you know that the only reason I'm doing this is because Momma Linda asked me too! That's it! But anyway. Call now while my man not here.

Charlotte immediately did so.

"It's me, Shug!"

Charlotte was reduced to tears at the sound of Shug's voice. Her sobs were heard through the phone. She made her way to the bathroom to hold a private conversation. Charlotte knew that no matter what had taken place in their lives, Shug still had a soft spot for her, anytime emotion was displayed. "Shug . . . please forgive me for anything I've done to offend you. Okay? I beg of you please forgive me," Charlotte said.

"Talk, Carmen. Because my time is limited," Shug responded.

"Look. You already know that the only reason I did what I had, was because I was on the verge of going to prison for a long time, and they were going to take my baby away from me. Not to mention, I didn't get the chance to tell you about the full situation that was going on between my cousin and Vershon."

"Carmen. So you mean to tell me that there wasn't a better way you could've handled the overall situation? I mean for real! You a whole cold-blooded rat now, girl! There's no way you could ever change that!"

"Well, if that's who I've gotta be for saving me, my baby, you, your man, and everybody else, then, I'm fine with that. And besides, Vershon was the only one to get locked up and go off to prison. He *got* what he deserved. That motherfucka shot my cousin in the head right there in front of me! This came after he'd beat me nearly to death. And, getting my cousin Misty pregnant. They got a son together now. But let everybody else tell it, I'm the foul one! Never mind Karma coming around to get him, huh!" Charlotte stated.

"You make sense with most of what you just said. But truth be, you knew what you was getting into at the time when you first met the man. Anyway, how you been?" Shug finally asked.

"Life has been pretty good moving forward. For the most part. What about you?"

"Me and Breezy been fine through the years. Just living life."

"So what all you do now? Work wise?"

"I own a hair and beauty supply shop. But please, don't get too comfortable asking me too many goddamn questions. It ain't no telling *what* you still got going on!"

"That's good. But me, I'm in the medical field actually. An NP," Charlotte made her aware.

"An NP! What the hell is that?" retorted Shug.

"A Nursing Practitioner. It's a top position at the hospital where I work."

"Oh. A nurse. I don't even wanna ask in what city. Because I'm sure you're not at liberty to speak on that."

"No. I'm not. At least not at this time. But I promise to soon. You know you're my sister, Shug. Always have been. Always will be. No matter what," Charlotte declared.

"Likewise. But I'm still pissed, Carmen. Very much so. Hopefully, I'll get over it at some point soon. But for right now, it's not likely."

The two continued to talk for a time longer. They made attempts to mend their fractured relationship to the best of their ability. And this came about by Shug hearing Charlotte's side of the story. Her message was conveyed in a shrewd way, trying to place Shug in the mind frame to question what would *she* had done if faced with the same situation? Women always had an excellent way of making another woman feel where they are coming from. This was exactly what Charlotte had done.

They came to an agreement to meet down in Trinidad, in the next month to come. This would be to celebrate Charlotte's mother's sixtieth birthday bash. Everything will then come out while the two are to be face-to-face.

***

The next day, Murder, Charlotte, and Ni'Asia visited the home of the Appletons. While Murder and Major played pool and entertained one another over games of chess and target practice with the pellet guns again, Charlotte, Lori and their daughters took a tour of Philly. They shopped, made rounds to the business establishments owned by the Philadelphia Charter of Sorority Sisters whom Charlotte was looking to be acquainted with, and ate at a restaurant owned by Lori. She was a known and respected face around town. Mostly due to the husband being a public figure.

Through the online search of a home by Charlotte and Lori, one was noticed. Charlotte took a liking to it. The house was located in a posh Germantown neighborhood. There was an array of other homes present with well-manicured lawns as was the one Charlotte favored. It was a two-story mini mansion with an asking price of seven hundred fifty-four thousand. The money to buy the place wasn't an issue. This was partly why Charlotte wanted to take a trip to Trinidad, to retrieve the funds to buy the home. However, she figured if she could get Barry to pay for everything, the better for her and her daughter. And more than likely, she may be able to convince him to meet her halfway. But with Charlotte being of high maintenance, she disliked the idea of being met only halfway. With her, it was all the way or no way at all! This was her motto.

Charlotte absolutely liked Murder and knew what could be done to have him foot the bill in totality. She wanted her cake and ice cream together. Her version of a sweet combination of pleasing treats that was to last a lifetime.

An in-person tour of the home was requested. A deposit would soon follow. Charlotte was making progress in her transition. Her connection to Lori was proving to be worthwhile.

***

One Week Later . . .

Murder was sure to show Charlotte and Ni'Asia a very good time during their visit. The home chosen by Charlotte appealed to him as well. He really appreciated the level of safety and diverse reflection of the neighborhood where the home was located. It wasn't hood by any stretch of the imagination.

The particular agreement that Murder and Charlotte came to was that he would pay for the home himself, so long as both their names was to go on the deed, and that neither of the two could do nothing with the place without both of their signatures to authorize action.

Murder wanted to proceed in this way so as to keep him with full access to the house, to come and go like he saw fit, and to also add the property to his portfolio. He thought ahead to keep himself at an advantage. Charlotte made no argument about anything.

For the particular weekend that was upon Murder, he wanted to share it with Felicia. The business with his drug operation was flowing smoothly and this afforded him the time away to get back acquainted with her. Every man deserves the luxury of leeway. This is so to balance work and the personal life.

He booked a two-day reservation at the Ritz-Carlton Hotel, and this was perfect for what Felicia had in mind. She desired quality time with Murder so as to relish in those strong feelings all over again that was once held in high school between the two. She didn't really want to be out in public for fear of being observed by a coworker, or worse, someone who knew she was a federal prosecutor. It was too risky. And the more they were inside an establishment, the better. Also, the current boyfriend Felicia had in her life, Gregory Conner, wasn't so satisfying to her sexually. Not as she knew Murder to be. Greg, being the opposite, was a rigid personality and not fun. All he did was work and performed no play. Not Felicia's cup of tea.

To sum it up, Felicia would be perfectly fine lounging around in the hotel suite the whole weekend with Murder. Besides, The Ritz-Carlton had a spa and many other luxury accommodations to make her time worthy.

The two fucked like they never had before over the weekend. Murder climaxed at least five times throughout those three days, and Felicia, maybe more. The flame of love and passion was rekindled between them.

Chapter 17

Dollar Bill made it his business to contact his beloved daughter, Tatiana. He needed her to come by his place to speak with her about something. The issue was urgent and required a face-to-face discussion. He had a doctor's appointment and wanted Tati to take him.

There was no amount of danger to threaten her to keep her away from her daddy. She loved him. The dope-head Dollar Bill and all to come along with it. She was committed to helping her father become a better man, no matter the cost or the consequences.

"Hey, Daddy," Tatiana answered.

"Hey there, baby. How you doing?" Dollar Bill responded.

"I'm fine, Daddy. And I'm sorry I ain't been by to see you in a while. But I will soon. I've got a few problems to take care of before I'm able to."

"But what if I told you, I really need to see you? Besides, I've got a doctor's appointment today at two, and I need you to come take me. You already know I ain't got nobody else to care for me like this," Dollar Bill expressed in a sympathetic voice.

Tatiana paused in her speech to think over a few things. she then offered a response.

"Look. I'll be by, Daddy. This is just a chance I've gotta take. I don't have no fear of showing my face. And you're my daddy. I've gotta help you out."

"That's how I like to hear you talk, baby. Daddy didn't raise you to be no scary girl, no matter what you got going on," Dollar Bill stated.

He had no idea who his daughter had a beef with.

"I'll be there at one o'clock today, Daddy. You know I ain't never lied to you," Tatiana replied.

The time was 10:00 A.M.

"Okay, baby. I'll be here," Dollar Bill lastly said.

The call between the two concluded.

Tatiana had a general idea of what her father really wanted to talk about in person, as she was aware of his health issues. He actually did have an appointment to make, and it was a must he do so.

"How was that? Did I do good?" Dollar Bill said with a smile on his face.

He was talking to his nephew . . . Murder, who was there with him. Dollar Bill's phone was on speaker as he spoke to his daughter. The twin sister Karen, and Quana were there as well. Karen wanted to put an end to the foolishness that her and Dollar Bill's kids had going on.

"Yes, Kev. You did great, bro," Karen said.

"Because we can't sit back and continue to allow our kids to destroy themselves or us with this nonsense they got going on."

"Yeah Unk. That was good. I liked that. And as promised, here you go," Murder said, then peeled away two one hundred-dollar bills from the roll he had.

"Tati believes any and everything you say to her, don't she, Uncle Kev?" Quana chimed in to say. "And that was a good way to get her to listen."

Murder now proceeded to tell the others what the plan was moving forward.

"A'ight look. Quana, you and Momma go on ahead and take y'all place back at my pad until it's time. I'mma call at twelve-thirty. Tati said she'll be here at one. I'mma make a few runs and take care of some business between the time., me and Dollar Bill. I know he won't mind riding around with me and we go out to eat a decent meal."

"I damn sho' won't, nephew. This has to be an act of God, for you to consider me this type of way," Dollar Bill let out.

Everyone had to laugh behind his words.

They all agreed to the plan in place and went about their way.

***

Prior to the day, while Quana was in Maryland, with Karen and Murder over in D.C. with Charlotte, Quana related everything to her mother about what was going on between her and Tatiana. Karen questioned Murder concerning the issues while he visited one day. He confirmed all his sister had already brought to their mother's attention. This became the moment he came up with the brilliant idea to rid him and Quana of the problems they had, with Heeme at the center of it all.

Murder was a cold-hearted nigga no doubt, but he couldn't push himself to take the life of his own flesh and blood. He couldn't so much as harm Tatiana no type of way, as he knew, if anything bad was to happen to his cousin, it would absolutely destroy his mother and her twin. So, to compromise what he'd been ordered to do, he formulated another plan to offer Tatiana once he had her trapped in Dollar Bill's apartment. He needed Dollar Bill to play along. And that's where Karen came in at. To deal with her twin.

Murder had his mother explain the situation to Dollar Bill. He knew if it wasn't anybody else in the world, Dollar Bill would listen to Karen, and wouldn't question a thing. This became the overall intention, to have the twins straighten out their kids. And once this was to be done, then get themselves straightened out. For good, possibly. With no looking back.

***

The time reached 12:50 P.M. Tatiana showed up ten minutes earlier than she said he would. She had a key to her father's place and let herself through the first door to the stairway that led to the door of the apartment. She then opened it and was now inside the living space.

"Daddy! Where you at? I'm here!" She called out for Dollar Bill.

"Hey! I'm back here in my room. Trying to finish getting dressed. Come on back, will you? I'm putting on my after shave and deodorant, baby," Dollar Bill responded.

"Ok, I'm on my way back there now," Tati let out then began to make steps through the short hallway that led to the bedroom.

She took notice of her father seated on the bed attending to himself as he said he was.

Murder allowed Tatiana enough time to get fully inside and enter the bedroom, before he eased out of the closet in the living room and followed right behind her footsteps. She never heard him creeping up, as Dollar Bill had her to take a seat on the bed alongside him, as if he were ready to have a brief discussion.

Murder casually eased himself to the doorway of the room, with his pistol in the palm of his hand, but held it behind his back so as to not be seen. Tati's head was low with her face planted on the screen of her cellphone. She toyed around with the keyboard to make a post on social media. She never raised her head once to look up. Not until her name was called out.

"How you doing, Tati?" Murder let out.

He had his long frame propped against the door panel of the room. Tatiana recognized the voice and raised her head frantically to know whether or not it was who she thought it was.

"Huh!" she gasped in fear. Scared beyond all her days.

Her eyes bucked as she looked on at Murder in a petrified state of being. Her mouth widened. And she now were in fear of her life being endangered. Tatiana had no words to come up to be said. She anticipated all that he might have to say.

"You surprised to see me? Yeah. I'm sure you are. Just relax. I ain't gonna do nothing to you. I just wanna talk, actually," Murder said in a very calm and easy way.

He honestly didn't want her to be afraid of him.

"What is it you want, Barry?"

"What is it I want?" he retorted. "I actually want this family to come to its goddamn senses and be peaceful towards one another again. That's what I want. For you two hot in the ass bitches—you and Quana—to kill all the bullshit y'all got going on behind some sorry-ass nigga!" Murder stated.

"How did you get in here? Because I know I locked both doors."

"Tati, I was already in here by the time you arrived. Me and your daddy already had an agreement worked out. Uncle Kev helped set up the whole thing," Murder revealed.

Tatiana whisked her head to the right to look on at her father. "Daddy! You helped set this up for Barry to creep up on me like this?"

"I did, I did. Because me and Karen gotta do what we gotta do to help see you kids back straight again. We need peace once more. This family not how family 'pose to act towards one another, Tatiana. And if it required me to set you up for us to talk, then be it may," Dollar Bill declared.

"Daddy! How could you! Now what if Barry was trying to kill me? Then what?"

"—Then you'd be dead already. I would think. So relax. All I wanna do is make peace. And to also offer a compromise," Murder injected rapidly.

Murder then placed his pistol in his back pocket. Tatiana didn't notice a thing. He pulled his phone from his hip clip and texted Quana and told her and Karen to now make their way to the apartment. They weren't too far away. The two were situated in Brooklyn's car at a Popeye's Chicken down Broad Street. Quana was able to move about town in a more comfortable state of mind and undisturbed by any thoughts of Heeme retaliating.

Murder got back to the discussion with Tatiana.

"Okay, look. Here's the deal Tati. The little issue between you and Quana, the one you was supposed to take care for me alone, you fucked up. You fucked up big time, you hear me!? And ain't but one way to fix it."

"And what about this mess with me and Quana over a nigga we're both in love with?" Tati asked.

"Man, please! Don't even worry about that shit! She'll be here shortly for us to work things out. Besides, that's the least of our worries compared to the other shit. And I hope you're ready to have a fist fight with Quana at least, so as to end y'all's pettiness. Because I'm gonna have to ask her what does she want to happen to dead this beef you two going at each other with. And me knowing her, she may wanna throw hands. Do a fade or something with you," Murder stated with a chuckle.

He knew if anything, Quana would want to fight and max Tatiana out with a good ass-whipping. It was only right that she would want to conclude their problems this way and not in dramatic fashion as before.

"Well, whatever you kids do to get things back right again, just do what y'all gotta do. Just don't cut, shoot, or kill one another please. That's all I ask," Dollar Bill said.

"Nah, Unk. We good. I'mma be sure that things go smoothly."

"Yeah, Daddy. We're good."

"Well then, I'm good. And it's all good, because the Fredrick's family shall continue to be good. So help us God," Dollar Bill proclaimed.

Almost twenty minutes later, Quana and Karen were now at the front door. Quana called to notify him.

Murder had Dollar Bill go down to let them in. With Dollar Bill momentarily out the way, this allowed an opportunity for Murder and Tatiana to privately speak.

"Tati. The dude whose truck you borrowed that day. What's his name?"

"LaShawn. That's his name. LaShawn Norton," she replied.

"Okay. Well, the bottom line to it all is, he's gotta go. He's the link between you and the case. According to my sources, Philly Homicide looking for you to question. That's why we've gotta act fast to get rid of Holmes, before the cops go back to him for more information. You gotta set his ass up. Today, Tati. Then, take his ass out! Or else, you go to jail. Quana goes to jail. I go to jail. And a whole bunch of other shit will fuck around and become exposed. And I can't have that happen. Because that'll then put me in a predicament where I won't have no choice but to kill you. And I don't wanna do that, but I will if I have to. You understand all I'm telling you?" stated Murder.

"Yes, Barry. I understand. I know this has to be serious for you to threaten me like that," Tati responded in a somber tone of voice.

She then began to mull over in fear the worst-case scenario. The one of her own cousin having to kill her.

Quana, Karen, and Dollar Bill now stood in the presence of the other two. Quana looked on at Tati with an angry face. She then snarled at her, displaying a fang in the process. It was a surreal moment to be remembered by them all. They began to try and gauge the energy of one another so as to know intentions. Different emotions radiated individually as heads rotated from one to the other. Tatiana honestly didn't know what to make of the situation. There was simply too much on her plate to sort out. Problems she created for herself.

Tatiana needed to absolve herself of the dire predicament she was now faced with. And this needed to happen quickly.

"Well, ain't you two gonna at least say hello to one another?" Karen said, referring to Quana and Tati.

"You know what, Momma," Quana began, looking in Tati's direction as she spoke. "I'm smart enough to know that I've got to be the bigger person of the two. Hello, Tati. How you doing, cuz?" she said, her voice was humble and non-threatening.

"Hey, Quana. I'm doing ok. Hopefully we can reconcile our differences today and move past the bull-ish we've got going on," Tatiana responded.

"To be real with you, it wouldn't have ever come to this, had you went out and found your own man, and left mine alone."

The two girls caused the heads of the other three to go from one to the other as they exchanged comments.

Quana continued. "An apology would be good to keep everything flowing in the right direction."

"Quana. I'm sorry, ok? I never meant for us to fall out like this. I was wrong. Will you please find forgiveness in your heart and let's move on?" Tati asked.

"That's not a problem. I can do that. I forgive you, Tati. And yes, we can move on. However, I'mma still want a fade with you though. I've gotta beat that ass the first chance I get to do so! A fair fight. One-on-one. Okay?"

"Now, Quana. We both are too grown to be fighting. And you know this. We've got too much other stuff to concern ourselves with than to be going back and forth about Heeme. So can we please just move forward and get back to getting along like a family truly supposed to? I apologized already." Tatiana spoke her peace for a second time.

"Well, y'all kids listen up for a moment. Me and Karen about to have Quana take me to my doctor's appointment. And from this point moving forward, we both want you kids on y'all best behavior, now that we've kissed and made up. Y'all got that," Dollar Bill stated. He then gathered what he needed and he, Karen, and Quana made their way out the door, leaving Murder and Tatiana once more.

Murder got back to the topic they needed to talk about.

"A'ight, look. Now that we got the small shit out the way, it's on to the other. Quana not gonna come for you no more. Even though she does want smoke about that nigga Heeme, I'm not gonna allow nothing more to pop off. Because it's over with between her and dude. For you and him too, Tati. That bitch-ass nigga gotta go! That's all there is to it. I've got my hound dogs on the loose already, trying to track his ass down. But enough on him, we've got bigger shit to concern ourselves with. Because I'm gonna utilize you to kill two troubles at one time. The LaShawn nigga *and* Heeme. If my hitters don't get to him first," Murder stated.

"I'm with you, Barry. What has to be done, has to be done," Tatiana responded.

"Like I've made you aware of, there's a sense of urgency to the LaShawn thing. It has to happen today. We can't afford for dude to still be breathing by the time the sun rises in the morning. Do I make myself clear?"

Murder was determined to help Tatiana understand the severity of the situation.

"I know this is serious business, Barry. I realize what I've gotta do."

"Whack LaShawn! That part, right?"

"Yes, whack LaShawn! That part indeed," Tatiana retorted.

"Do I need to send Quana with you to do this?" Murder asked. He couldn't afford anymore fuck-ups.

"For what? So she could try to fight me the moment we're all alone! Nah! I'm good. I'll be able to set him up, then do what I need to do on my own."

"You sure? Because this can't go sideways like the last one, Tati. No more room for errors," Murder stated emphatically.

"I'm positive, Barry. I can handle it."

"Well, say no more. Here," he said, then withdrew a roll of money. Murder gave her a thousand dollars. "And if you can, catch that nigga down bad while he's at home or something. Put him in a comfort zone mentally, then hit him. Slit his throat with a knife or a razor instead of shooting him. It's quieter and leaves less evidence. No gun powder residue or bullets to be traced back." Murder was sure to provide specific instructions.

Tatiana looked on at her cousin with a paranoid demeanor, took the cash he offered and put it away into her purse.

Everything was now in place to begin the clean-up Tatiana originally made. Once complete with taking out LaShawn, they all could continue to move forward without any more static from the cops and their investigation. This was only if all was to go well.

Chapter 18

Hours Later . . .

Tatiana went to her place over in West Philly. Throughout the time, she thought over all that had already taken effect. She found it difficult to fathom the predicament that she was now in. How ugly was her reality. Had she simply not accepted Murder's money to kill the pregnant girl, maybe things would've been better off. But it didn't happen that way. And the duty was now upon her to do a thing which she'd only seen done, but never carried out on her own. That was to take the life of another. With no other choice in the matter. Or it would be hers that would be taken.

She knew Murder wouldn't hesitate to kill her at this point, if she refused to terminate LaShawn, or fucked up once more. A thought passed through her mind. *I wonder how Barry knows all he do about LaShawn. I may never know, I'm sure.* She then sucked her teeth and proceeded with the plan.

Tatiana contacted LaShawn on her personal phone. She was surprised to know he hadn't disconnected the number, although she'd changed the one she previously had.

Reluctant to answer from a number he didn't recognize, he finally did so, thinking maybe it was some business that needed his attention.

"This is LaShawn!"

"Hey, LaShawn. How you been?"

Tatiana utilized her sensuous voice, which she knew he'd go for.

"Tatiana!"

"Yes. This me. How you doing?"

"I've been good. But I don't think it's a good idea for me to be speaking with you. It may cause me more problems with the cops. They looking for you too," he said.

"Speaking to me may cause you more problems with the cops! They looking for me!" she retorted. "Boy, stop with the foolishness. How is that?" Tatiana retorted.

"There's a lot I can't say to that." But for the record, I ain't have nothing to do with somebody being killed!"

"Well, what I used your truck to do was for what I said I would do. That's it. And how did you find out Philly Homicide was looking for me to question, if they really are? Why you just now bringing this to my attention? I deserve to know, I thought," Tatiana responded.

"I didn't say anything to you because I was told by the cops not to contact you. That's why. They're still investigating," LaShawn stated.

"And you chose to listen to them before you brought it to my attention? The one you say you love. The one you're fucking. And the person you promised to protect. Really, LaShawn!"

She worded things in a way to cause him to feel bad for not letting her know sooner.

"And whether you know it or not, those people are really trying to frame you, LaShawn! Think for a moment, will you. They say your truck was used. Whoever the girl was, so happened to be the niece of the mayor. And, more than likely, there's video somewhere of you as an activist for what you believe in and stand for. Like you protesting at those Black Lives Matter vigils. The cops could easily frame you for the murder. But then, you could counter that with the videos and accuse them for harassing you behind your activism. They could be acting out of vengeance against you—the company you work for I'm speaking of—to cover up something deeper associated with them. A scandal of some sort. Just think for a moment, if you will," Tatiana stated.

She spoke a whole lot of mumbo-jumbo to cause LaShawn to think in many other ways other than her being guilty of something. Maybe her play would work, by taking the blame off of her, and redirecting it someplace else. A classic form of reverse psychology.

"You make a good point, Tatiana. Those bastards did suspend me pending their investigation. And if my truck was there like they claim it was, they would've made me the main suspect. Not anyone else."

Tatiana thought over his statement.

But how the fuck did the cops come to the conclusion to name me as a suspect? This nigga had to have mentioned my name to them. I'mma just keep quiet and let him talk more, to see what all he knows. I can talk around the subject, while he continues to talk on the subject.

"And your black ass would be locked up by now if this were true!"

"You're right. You're so right. They wouldn't have never let me go free from custody. I apologize to you. When can I see you again so we may talk about this in person?"

"That's the main reason I called. So we could hook up and go out on a date or something. I wanted to see you. But a date won't be possible now, since you just let me know that the cops are looking for me to question. I don't wanna be arrested."

"Well, can I at least come by your place? I wouldn't mind seeing you," asked LaShawn of her.

"I'm cool with seeing you. And I think it'll be best if you stop by to pick me up, and let's get a hotel room over in Jersey to spend time together. How does that sound?"

"Sounds like a win-win situation to me. I've got to see you. And I want us to have the opportunity to spend quality time together. So, I'll be by shortly to pick you up," he said.

"Don't have me waiting too long. I'm about to pack a bag now, ok?"

The call between the two came to an end.

Roughly an hour later, LaShawn was pulling up to Tatiana's house to pick her up. She was already packed and ready to roll for a few days of fun with him. She exited the house and got into his SUV. He had a new model Acura.

"Hello, LaShawn! I'm so glad you made time for me," she greeted with a smile.

The two tongue-kissed.

"I'm glad myself to be able to spend time with you as well, Tatiana. I feel special to have someone like you in my life," he responded.

They pulled off, en route to Cherry Hill, New Jersey to check into a room.

LaShawn registered the suite under his name. The intention was to go out for a meal and a movie, then return. However, strong sexual urges took hold of LaShawn, as he was ready to have some of the goodness the biracial beauty had between her legs. And not only that. Tatiana didn't see the need to waste time to do what she knew had to be done. The sooner she could fuck him and put dude to sleep, the better. Kill him, then get the hell on back to Philly.

LaShawn wrapped his arms around Tati's body as they sat on the bed and watched TV.

"Tatiana, if only you knew how much I missed you," he whispered in her ear.

"Mmm-hmm! Is it me that you missed? Or is it the good loving from my wet pussy and bomb-ass head I give you?" She put her sexual banter to use.

"That too!" he responded, batting his eyes and waggling his index finger towards the ceiling.

"Well what's the hold up? If fucking is what you wanna do, LaShawn, to help get the monkey off your back and make up for the time, then just say that, ok," Tatiana said to him.

She wanted dude to be more direct with what he wanted. A trait LaShawn always struggled to overcome.

"Ok. No problem, Tatiana. I wanna fuck right here right now, to get the monkey off my back and make up for lost time between us, because I miss that pretty pussy you got, and the head you give," he expressed in a playful manner, causing her to erupt in laughter. Something he was always good at.

Tatiana then thought back over the seriousness of the situation and put play to the wayside.

"Now that's more like it, sweetie. Come here," she let out.

They began to tongue kiss like they were crazy in love. The undressing followed. Next thing you know, the two were all the way into the midst of things, fucking like jack rabbits.

The thrill didn't last long, maybe four minutes. LaShawn blew his load onto her belly and on the inner thigh area of the mixed hottie. At times, Tati would allow him the pleasure of releasing inside of her. But she hadn't taken any birth control shots in a while, and wanted to reserve this type of satisfaction for Heeme, if she wasn't already pregnant. She'd missed her period that was supposed to have begun days prior.

They went to the bathroom and washed up together. Following that, they sat atop the bed in the nude and continued to watch TV.

"LaShawn, honestly, I'm not up for going out while we spend time together. If that's ok with you? I just wanna relax here like we are and continue to do what we do. Can we do that, please?"

"I'm fine with that, Tati. This about all I wanted to do anyway. Chill," LaShawn said.

"You want me to massage your back like I always do?"

"That'll be nice. Come on with it. I could really use that right about now."

Tati got up from the bed and went over to the carry-all tote bag she brought along. She withdrew two objects, a bottle of baby oil, and another object to do additional work with. She returned to the bed, being sure not to let LaShawn take notice of the other object she had. Taking a seat, she situated her back against the head area of the bed.

"I want you to relax, LaShawn. I'm gonna make you feel real good after this, ok?" she said.

"Now that part! Making me feel real good. You've already done that part. At least for the moment," LaShawn responded.

He then lay flat on his chest and looked in the opposite direction. Tatiana procrastinated no longer with the business. Her plan was well thought out as she took a quick shower when they both washed up after sex. LaShawn didn't stay in as long as she had.

With tears welled up in her eyes, she eased her hand under the thick pillow she was propped upon to grab hold of the box-cutter. A new blade was inserted before he'd picked her up. The silent killing tool was gripped tightly in her palm. Tatiana was in the process of taking LaShawn out exactly how Murder told her to, by slitting his throat. However, she didn't move fast enough, and fate didn't have it in the plans for him to die that day.

Wham!

The door to the hotel was knocked clean from its hinges by a police battering ram.

"Cherry Hill and Philadelphia Police! Freeze!" the cops yelled at the same time. "You're under arrest! Put your hands where we can see them!"

They barked their orders loud and clear. Both LaShawn and Tatiana's hands were held high above their heads.

"Drop that weapon you have in your hands, ma'am!" the lead officer sternly ordered Tatiana.

LaShawn turned his head to have a look at the weapon the cop was referring to. The razor slid from her palm down to the mattress blanket. He looked on at Tatiana with his mouth wide as ever. LaShawn was in total disbelief at what he came to realize. There was an evil intent to kill him. And right at the last minute, the deed he'd done while she was in the shower, was the thing to save his life.

On the flip side of things, Tatiana was shocked at the presence of the police. She began to question in her own mind how did they know exactly where she could be found? The truth of the situation would reveal itself in due time.

"The both of you are under arrest! Anything you say can and will be used against you in a court of law . . . ."

Their Miranda rights were being read to them as the handcuffs were locked onto their wrists. While restrained and seated atop the bed, in walked the lead detective from Philly Homicide, along with an investigator of the Cherry Hill Police Department. The deed LaShawn had done was contact the Philly Investigator Watson Porter and made him aware that the female they wanted regarding the Shavika Felton murder, was there at the hotel with him as they spoke. And he would preoccupy her for the time being until they arrived. Porter provided LaShawn his card when they questioned him. He needed LaShawn's cooperation to help set up Tatiana.

Porter gave an order to the arresting officers. "Uncuff the guy, leave her detained," he said, pointing a finger from one to the other.

Tatiana knew then and there she'd been crossed out.

"LaShawn! How could you!" she let out.

"It was one of two choices, Tatiana. Me or you. And I for damn sure wasn't gonna go to jail for something I didn't do, for something that you've done. I'm innocent!" he responded.

"Tatiana Fredricks, you're under arrest for the murder of Shavika Felton!" stated Porter.

"We had a hard time trying to figure out who you were and how to track you down. It's a good thing your boyfriend here made the right decision."

"LaShawn, you ain't shit! *Ptui!*" Tatiana said, then spit in the guy's face. "You lame, cornball-ass nigga! You're gonna get what's coming to you! I promise you that! I should've not wasted so much time and slit your fucking throat when I had the chance to, pussy!"

She went on-and-on until they finally had her ass in the car and en route to the county jail in Philly.

To add further insult to injury, the cops put an additional charge on Tati, one for terroristic threats to go along with the capital murder count. Her status was upgraded from questioning to prime suspect. She was in for a long process ahead of her.

With Tatiana being arrested, the situation brought along so much to go about in the many problems she faced. There were simply too many issues. And now with her being on the verge of being convicted and going to prison for the brutal slaying of a pregnant female, it was only a matter of time before the cops were to approach her about Shavika's death and she started spewing to them all they might need to know regarding the investigation. The days were numbered for Murder and Quana on the streets as free persons, if their cousin was to say anything to the cops.

Chapter 19

One Day Later . . .

Murder made several attempts to contact Tatiana to no avail. He tried her phone number, her Messenger account, Instagram, Snapchat, and email. She could not be reached. He became so pissed behind the thought of his cousin maybe playing him for a fool yet again, that he began to regret not killing her as Jabari told him to. He fumed vehemently.

I can't allow this bitch the chance to go on now without me finally putting an end to her and all the clown shit she got going on! It's a must now that I kill this slimy bitch! he thought.

Murder called up Quana to know if or not she had any knowledge of Tati's whereabouts.

"What's up, bro!" she answered.

She and Karen was at his penthouse for the time being, while he camped out at the home in Lower Marion, babysitting all the many kilos of product he had left.

"I don't know why I find myself asking you this, but, that slimy bitch Tati, you have any idea where she may be?" Murder asked.

"Bro! I'mma keep it a buck with you, a'ight. Once we found out that that bitch was no good, and I put you in the fucked-up predicament I had by shooting at her and Heeme, we should've waxed that bitch then and there! That would've been the best thing to have done. Had that happened, we wouldn't be in the particular situation we are now, where we've gotta track this bitch down again, only to give her another extension on life. But to answer your question. You know if you haven't seen or heard from her, I haven't either."

Quana was sure to respond in her signature sarcastic way.

"Enough said, sis. Say no more. I'm only hoping the bitch has handled the particular business she was supposed to take care of. That's all."

"And if she hasn't?"

"Then that only means we've got another person on the list to be dealt with—"

"You mean a bitch we *should've* been dealt with, don't you! A long time ago," Quana cut him off to say.

"Look, you gonna keep beating me up about it, or are we in the process of trying to find out what the bitch got going on and put an end to it? Long before it comes back to harm us!"

"You know I'm with you all the way, bro. I just need for you to get back to being cold-blooded and stop playing with motherfuckers! Stop letting shit slide so much! Especially the shit you need to put an end to. It's like you've gotten soft, bro, ever since you been dating that Charlotte chick. And you're too gangsta' for that. To continue and compromise. Real talk!"

Quana made sure to speak her mind and voice her concerns to her brother. She worded things in a way he'd clearly understand. Out of all the people in his life, Quana was probably the only one who had the leeway to talk to him like she had. Without having to bite her tongue.

"Humph! I never thought of myself in that way. But I guess it must be some degree of truth to it, if it's coming from you. I'll be sure to keep your words in mind, sis. I need people like you to put me on point anytime I'm slipping," he responded.

Quana kept silent and allowed Murder the opportunity to have the last word. He was bad about that.

"I'll hit you again later, ok? I've gotta make a few more calls to find out what may be going on."

Quana was hit by an impulse to respond to those words.

"And this time when we finally do track this bitch down, please let me do what needs to be done and put her lights! For good! Ok? May I please have that pleasure to do that? It'll be for the old and the new," she responded.

"I'm gone, Quana. Talk later."

The call ended.

Murder next contacted Traino. He wanted an update on his search seeking to locate Heeme. No luck as of yet.

***

Once Tatiana was booked and her bail denied at the first appearance, she made it her business to contact her father, to let him know the situation. She needed Dollar Bill to get in touch with Karen, and for her to reach out to her son, for him to offer help legally. A lawyer was necessary. Court appointed representation wouldn't do with the type of situation she had.

"Hello!" Dollar Bill answered.

"Daddy! It's me, Tatiana, I'm in jail! I need you to call Karen, and tell her to contact Barry, to let him know I need help," she started.

"You in jail! Baby! What in the devil going on now?"

"I can't talk about it right now, Daddy. In fact, I don't wanna talk about it."

"Well at least tell me what they got you charged with?"

"Murder, Daddy! I've been charged with murder. So look, call Mommy for me too and tell her what's going on. I need her to put some money on the phone so I can call. Somebody in here gave me a three-way. I tried to call Mommy already. She's not picking up. And I may not be able to call for a couple days."

"Goddamn, baby! This too much on your pop! But ok, I'm about to make those calls for you now. You be safe up in there, and take care of yourself, you hear? Daddy loves you too!" Dollar Bill said.

"I love you too, Daddy. Bye-bye."

The call came to an end between the two.

Dollar Bill immediately took on the task of contacting the people his daughter needed him to get with. He was now worried out of his mind over his one and only. Not long before the day, the heavy burden of stress and depression of the man was lifted from his shoulders. And just like that, the same was upon him yet again. What was a man like him to do?

***

Upon a recent visit to the doctor's office, it was revealed to Dollar Bill that the previous physician made the terrible mishap of providing the wrong test results to him. What happened was that Dollar Bill's blood work became mistakenly crossed up with that of another patient. A diagnosis of HIV infection was detected. The dreadful results was ascribed to the incorrect man, Dollar Bill Fredricks.

The new doctor appointed was asked to provide a second test and opinion, also not being the one to simply carry on with all another MD had done prior to him. Multiple vials of blood was drawn from Dollar Bill for a series of screenings, with much reluctance by the belligerent patient. Nonetheless, this was an act that later produced life, mind, and spiritual transformation in Dollar Bill.

At the conclusion of five separate test trails, it was determined that Dollar Bill was NEGATIVE regarding the virus, paving the way for a lawsuit against the first doctor to soon follow.

Now Dollar Bill faced a new battle. One that required him to put in his all in seeing to it his beloved daughter regained her freedom once more. He was ready to do all necessary to get Tatiana out of there.

Chapter 20

Herb now found himself doing well in the new line of business he was in alongside the Russians. He'd formulated a qualified crew of dealers who got rid of the product he was supplied, and now, he also had a cache of guns he sold in addition to the narcotics. Everything was courtesy of Vladimir. The weapons sold well themselves and opened the door to a totally different world for Herb. One he never knew.

On this particular day, a Monday and beginning of a work week, Herb had an appearance to make at the Federal District Court there in Philly. His presence wasn't needed behind any charges he'd caught at his own doing. But rather, at the behest of a male cousin of his, who'd been arrested and charged with four counts of firearms possession as a convicted felon. Herb was called upon to post bail for his people, if and when the bail was to be set.

He had a brief moment to talk with Imani as he sat inside his car, the Benz with gull wings to it, and awaited the 9:00 A.M. hour for the hearing to begin.

"Yeah, baby, I was able to find a nice house that we can begin buying at some point soon. Whenever you get here today, we can stop by the place and have a look at it. I'm more than sure you'll like it," Herb stated to the new girlfriend he now had in his life.

"How many bedrooms does it have, sweetie?" Imani asked.

144

It's a five bedroom, two and a half-bath joint. There's a pool in the backyard too, something I'm sure we'll grow to appreciate. Especially throughout these hot summer months. Being that it's now December, the value of the house is a lot lower than normal. We definitely need to go ahead and make our move before someone else does and we miss out on the home," Herb voiced what he thought regarding the importance to act fast on the purchase of the property.

"Ok, babe. I understand your point. I'm about two hours out from you now. I'll be there shortly."

"Ok. That's enough time to handle all I'm in the middle of. I'm at the courthouse. About to pay the bail fee for one of my people. He got himself jammed up in a little trouble with the law. But we gonna be a'ight though. He needed my help. So I had to come through for him."

"That's exactly what real men do, baby, take care of his lady and his people." Imani stated, stroking his ego for him.

"I appreciate your words too, sweetie. I really do. You make a difference to me and my life. Probably more than you may know at this point. But be sure to text me once you hit Philly, okay?"

"Okay, babe. See you shortly."

When the conversation ended, Herb exited the car and made steps towards the entrance of the court. The inside was filled with lawyers, prosecutors, one defendant who was awaiting the judge as he was the first of any to be called, and public spectators.

Within that sudden instance, Herb took notice of a face he believed he recognized. It was that of a Spanish female. Someone he hadn't seen in many years. Maybe since high school.

Is that who the fuck I think it is? He questioned himself.

The reason this particular woman managed to capture his attention in this way was because; one, she was seated on the prosecuting side of the aisle, at the table with the others who represented the government; and two, the female who he assumed it was, once had a deep affectionate relationship with his close friend and business partner, Barry. He was a guy who still to the day had a hand in on illegal activity in the underworld. This could potentially become troubling, if the two were to cross paths again and reunite—the female and his homie.

Herb now began to brainstorm in an attempt to remember whether or not Barry, aka Murder, mentioned of late anything about him reconnecting with the chick. Maybe he had, maybe he hadn't. Herb now wanted to be one hundred percent sure the female was who he thought she was before jumping to conclusions.

"All rise!" the bailiff called the court to order. "The Honorable Judge Ernest R. Campbell, presiding."

The entire audience of the court got to their feet.

"You may be seated," declared the judge. "The first case to be heard this morning is the United States versus Watson. A motion for bail is requested. Who is counsel on behalf of the government?" asked Judge Campbell.

"I am, your honor. AUSA Felicia Alvarez," stated the Spanish female prosecutor, the one Herb thought maybe he recognized. She then took her seat once more.

"What the fuck!" Herb let out from shock in a low voice. "I know damn well that that bitch Felicia, ain't a fed! My homie Murder, definitely gotta hear about this shit! I'm talking about like right now, he does."

Herb pulled his phone from the coat pocket, made sure that the silent mode was on, and texted Murder to inform on all he now had awareness of.

I had a good idea that it indeed was Felicia when I first lay eyes upon her. That's one thing I don't do, I never forget a face. It could cost me my life to make that type of mistake, he thought deeply to himself.

HERB: Yo bro! Yo not gonna believe this shit!

Shortly thereafter, Murder replied.

MURDER: What's that, bro?

HERB: How about your ex-girlfriend, the Puerto Rican hottie from back in the day Felicia is a fed now! The bitch is a prosecutor, bro!

MURDER: Nooo! How the fuck you find out all this? The both of us not too long ago reconnected. We back involved now. This can't be so.

HERB: The hell if it ain't! And if you got any sense, you better '*uninvolve*' yourself from the bitch, or suffer the consequences behind it.

Herb didn't pussy-foot around the issue any longer. He simply snapped a few photos of Felicia as she continued standing and addressing the court, then forwarded them to Murder.

HERB: Maybe these will help to convince you all the reasons more why you need to fall the fuck back from the bitch! And I'm talking ASAP!

Once Murder received the images and had a moment to react to himself, he responded to Herb.

MURDER: Wtf! The bitch did tell me she was a lawyer now and shit. But damn! A federal prosecutor. Nah.

HERB: I'm down at the fed court right now, bro. I'm waiting on my people to be called up for bail. My cousin Oskino.

Murder knew who the family member was Herb mentioned, and about the situation that led to him getting arrested.

MURDER: Word. Just hit me up later when you get the chance to. And I appreciate you putting me up on game too about Felicia. I plan to definitely ask her about it.

HERB: You already know how we rocking, bro. I'm down with you. Real talk.

Herb continued on with what he was in the process of doing, leaving Murder to do the same.

***

I don't believe this bullshit! Murder thought. He continued to look on at the photos of Felicia Herb sent.

This bitch is a motherfuckin fed! What the fuck! Ain't no way! No wonder she always seems to have a hard time letting me know where she lives or offering to invite me to her place. She's a prosecutor! It all makes sense to me now. It all makes sense. But here's what I'mma do. I'mma sit back and keep quiet about everything and utilize what I now know to my advantage. I'm the one who got the upper hand in it all. Also, I know the place where her father is being kept, just in case the bitch ever was to get all jazzy on me and try to pull off some slick shit about the line of work I'm into, Murder thought further.

A plot was already born inside Murder's mind on how he would strike back at Felicia if she ever decided to come for him. He then began to brainstorm in hindsight over all the conversations they'd had from the night at the club when they reunited.

Murder now wanted to know what all Felicia might know about him, or worse, had on him, being that her re-appearance was so sudden, and her eagerness for them to reunite so intense.

Damn, have I incriminated myself in any type of way? he thought. *Maybe I have. Maybe I haven't. Hell, I don't know. Who's to say?*

The reality of the situation was that Murder, had his head hung so far up Felicia's ass dating back to the night at the club, he had no idea on what all he might have said to her. An act that could potentially come back to bite him in the ass in federal court, the same stage where Felicia was now educated and trained to perform well on. The federal district court could turn out to be the burial ground for Murder through a legal process. One that a lover of his had the duty to dig for him. Things could get deep.

Prior to Herb texting, Murder was busy packing bags and preparing for the trip to Trinidad and Tobago. He and

Charlotte were to travel there for a vacation, and for him to finally have the opportunity to meet her family. Charlotte's mother had a birthday approaching later in the week. They were to celebrate. Charlotte was intent on reconnecting with Shug while there on the island nation. They had so much to discuss.

***

Murder was provided the bad news about his cousin Tatiana being arrested and charged with the murder of Shavika Felton. Throughout the time, he'd gotten two phone calls of serious nature. One was from his brother Jabari, and the other came from Major Appleton. They spewed their concerns about the potential backlash that could come their way behind the brutal killing of the Mayor's niece. The two men were more so pissed at Murder and the fuck-up he'd committed than anything. Had Murder simply taken care of the contract himself from the get-go, they wouldn't be at the point where they all now found themselves. But Murder's conscience wouldn't allow him to do the deed, no matter how cold-blooded he was at the time. Taking out a pregnant female was not something within the itinerary of Barry Murdoch.

On another note, he was set to be updated frequently on Tatiana and the situation she dealt with. And no doubt about it, he needed to have a conversation with her to know exactly all that happened on the day the victim was killed. What led the police to her to arrest? And what evidence did they have on her?

The LaShawn Norton witness was still alive for all Murder knew. There was now a need for him to find a way to kill the guy himself.

Tatiana gotta go too! so thought Murder.

She'd created too many problems and caused too much damage to be allowed the privilege to continue breathing.

Murder couldn't afford to even think about the possibility of her talking with the police. If she already hadn't. He had no idea.

Aside from the issues he faced with the threat Tatiana's arrest presented, and him trying like hell to find Heeme, things was going pretty well for Murder, especially so with the relations he had going with Charlotte and Brooklyn. The new developments about Felicia threw a monkey-wrench into the mix of all they had going. Upon his return from the Caribbean, he had it in mind to keep track of Felicia and dig deep into the life she now lived. He wanted to put her through the test of knowing how truthful she could be. This would be the determining factor to how he was to proceed with her moving forward. But having a girlfriend who was a federal prosecutor and wildly in love with him, was not a bad situation to be caught up in. All Murder would have to provide was love, time, attention, and understanding to her needs. How could he go wrong in this way?

Chapter 21

One Day Later . . .

Murder drove to Washington, D.C. to meet with Charlotte and Ni'Asia for the three of them to catch the flight out the country. Hours later they were there in the presence of the Margaux family.

Charlotte introduced the new boyfriend to everyone. Things went smoothly for the most part. And then, Murder began to have a difficult time understanding why every one of Charlotte's people was calling her by a different name than the one he knew. They referred to her as "Carmen," and he wasn't able to figure out why. Once the two of them got back to the hotel, he would definitely make it his business to question her about this. He couldn't do so at the present moment, because Charlotte had to return to the airport the same day to pick up Shug. The time alone between both of them was necessary, so to talk and air out whatever ill feelings they had against one another.

Charlotte was there at baggage claim to meet Shug. They stood twenty feet apart. There was a difference in Charlotte's appearance and demeanor to Shug. The cosmetic procedures and the professional position created the stark difference. Nonetheless, the nature of Charlotte's former life hadn't changed, as Shug knew all of Charlotte's favorite things.

Once they had the chance to lock eyes and observe each other, they simply stood in place and remained motionless. Each seemed afraid to make the first move. Finally,

Charlotte gave in, being that she operated as the co-host of the vacation.

"Hey Shug," she greeted. "How are you?"

Charlotte stepped closer.

Shug took a long pause before offering to reply. Her intention was to see would Charlotte continue in speech. She didn't, a degree of self-discipline was put to use. Shug then proceeded in a response.

"I'm fine, Carmen. What about yourself?"

"I'm well. Glad to see you was able to make it. I'm also glad you was grown enough to agree to meet with me, as we celebrate my mother's birthday this week, and for us to finally have the long-awaited conversation that's needed to be had," Charlotte said. She then rushed in to give Shug a loving hug. One that silently screamed, please forgive me, and love me again.

Tears welled up in Charlotte's eyes then streamed down her face. Still holding Shug in embrace, she kissed her on the lips. Shug returned the same show of affection, only with less emotion.

"As I said to you on the phone that time, Carmen, you got a lot of explaining to do. A lot!" Shug stated.

"How about, the both of us do. Because I know it was you who made the phone call to the feds to begin with. I heard the recording. I know it was you, Shug," Carmen fired back with.

"It may had been. It doesn't even matter now. But until we get to that point of where we'll do all the explaining to one another . . . I miss you, bitch! And I still love you," Shug let out with a smile. She felt the need to say something to throw off Carmen's attack on her, for pointing the finger at her about snitching, when she'd done the very same thing herself.

Charlotte turned into a little girl in that instance. So did Shug. They both grabbed hold of Shug's bags and headed to the car Charlotte rented.

On the ride from the airport, Charlotte related to Shug all about the new life now lived and of the new boyfriend, Barry. She spoke about the home in Philly they were soon to own, had shown off the huge diamond ring Barry gave to her, and went into discussion about Ni'Asia and how much she'd grown.

Shug managed to find much relief of her anger and frustration she'd held with Charlotte behind the level of honesty Charlotte was putting on display. All of the protocol the Witness Protection Program had in place to protect Charlotte was completely thrown to the wayside. She'd forgotten about any and all precautionary measures, and frankly didn't give a damn anymore at that point, until a time was to come when there was a need to do so. It was like nothing had changed between the two.

***

The two made their way to Charlotte's mother's home. Once there, they exited the car and entered the house. Mrs. Linda greeted Shug in her usual way she had through the years, as if she was her very own daughter. Shug was her "second born" daughter, she would say.

"Shug! Baby! I'm so happy you was able to make it. Momma Linda is pleased to see you again. It's been long enough. And from the looks of things, I assume you and Carmen were able to make things right between you two. I hope?" she said.

Murder had now heard the mother address Charlotte by the name "Carmen" one too many times. He now wanted to know why this was so? And right away. Charlotte had to be at the point in her mind to where she was ready to explain to him her past life and all that transpired to lead to the new one. Why else would she willingly expose him to her family and all that she knew they would refer to her as? And even if she wasn't, he was definitely ready to be let in on the secret.

"Charlotte, I need to speak with you for a moment please. In private," Murder whispered into her ear. This occurred before she had the chance to introduce him and Shug to one another.

"No problem, babe. Will do. Let's step outside for a moment. Maybe take a seat in the car and talk. I kinda got an idea what you wanna talk about. But I'mma leave that with you to say what you need to say," Charlotte responded.

As they made their way to the car, Murder went into the subject that he had on his mind.

"Help me out for a moment here, baby. Because I'm so confused."

"Ok. What you wanna know?"

"Now you told me your name was one thing . . . Charlotte. And yes, I know this to be true. But sweetie, I gotta know, why is everybody calling you Carmen? You care to let me in on that?" he asked.

Dude was already on edge about the issues his cousin Tatiana posed a threat with, and also made to fear the reality of his ex-girlfriend being a fed prosecutor. All of the above bothered him deeply. And now with the fact of his main girlfriend having two identities without giving him a heads-up why, he speculated greatly that there was a possibility that Charlotte or "Carmen," may indeed be a compliant witness in the federal Witness Protection Program. She only needed to confirm what he already suspected.

Charlotte looked on at Murder and sighed in a reluctant way. She then went on to properly explain to her man in clear terms what he wanted to know.

"Listen, Barry, okay? And you don't have to worry about me lying to you or not being fully open with what I know I need to tell you. I knew this day would come. And I'd long prepared in advance for the moment—"

"Will you please go on and let it out? Stop stalling," he cut in to say.

"Ok, look. Remember I gave you bits and pieces of information about my ex, right?"

"Yeah, I do. Ni'Asia's pops. But go ahead and get to the bread and meat for me please. Skip all the in between stuff for me. I like things to be straight and raw. Just spit it out," he urged her to do.

The reality of her situation and what Murder did for a living, made it difficult for her to simply "spit it out" like he told her to do. It wasn't that easy. What if he reacted in the wrong way behind her truth and then kill her and her daughter at some point afterwards? Charlotte took all of this into account. What if he no longer wanted anything to do with her moving forward? There was a lot at stake. They both had much on the line.

Charlotte shook her head slowly from side to side. "I knew I should've waited a little longer before I brought you all the way down here to meet my family, and truly know who I am. But my intentions was to keep things all the way—"

"If you don't go ahead and spit that shit out, I'mma really begin to think you got way more to hide than you letting on. Now get on with it, will you?" Murder demanded.

He was beginning to get angry now at Charlotte's procrastination. But his emphatic tone of voice and mean-mug facial expression caused her to get to the point.

"I'm in the federal Witness Protection Program, Barry! There you go. Now you know my secret. Anything else?"

Her bluntness matched the energy that he gave off.

Murder didn't immediately utter a word in response. He just continued to look on at her and clinch down on his teeth causing his jaw muscles to flex.

"I knew it was something like that about you. I fuckin' knew it! But here's what I definitely gotta know. You didn't rat on nobody, did you? Please don't tell me you're a snitch! Because that'll destroy me as a man and all I stand for in my line of work."

Charlotte returned the cold stare he gave to her, only she now had tears added into the mix at the thought of all she'd been through. She then came back with something emphatic of her own to say. "I ain't no motherfuckin' snitch! Let's get that part straight right now! And no, I didn't rat on nobody!" Her words had the sound of fury to them. She felt insulted.

"So what do you call it that you've done, in order to be a part of the Witness Protection Program?"

"I call it, doing what the fuck I needed to do, in order to save me and my daughter! That's what I call it. That nigga I was with was a monster! He turned out to be a no-good motherfucker!" Charlotte vented behind the thought of her ex.

"And I guess he got what he deserved too, huh?"

"You damn right, he did! A life sentence in prison!"

Murder took a pause so as to prevent the conversation from becoming ugly and leading to a fight between them two, potentially ruining the trip and drastically disrupting the plans for her mother's birthday celebration they had in store.

Murder had a question for her now. One he'd never asked. "What's the guy's name?"

He began to withdraw his phone and anticipated Charlotte's answer. The intention was to look the guy up on Google so to have a better knowledge of who he was, not to simply take her words for it any longer.

"His name is Vershon Aikens, aka 'Reign Man'."

Murder then performed his due diligence in researching the name and case on the mobile web.

"Hmmm! So your full born name I see is—"

"Carmen! Carmen Jenine Margaux! There. Now you know why everybody calls me that," she cut his words short to say.

"Why you gotta sound so spiteful and pissed off about it, sweetie? It's better we get this out the way now while we're into it than do so later. The timing of it all might not be good then like it is now. Don't you agree? But look, I ain't gonna be the boogeyman and spoil the happiness of our vacation.

So let's just wait until we get home to finish talking about this. At least we got the hard part out the way, right?" Murder stated. He honestly wanted to keep the situation as calm as could be. "I do have one last question though. Because I'm not sure what name do I call you by now. Charlotte still, or Carmen?"

Chapter 22

The first weekend in Trinidad for Charlotte and Murder turned out to be a busy one. She took on the responsibility to educate him on the culture of the country, on the traditional meals, and they were sure to attend the many festivities the country had to offer. Their Saturday was most memorable. They took photos and made videos to capture the moment. This also wound up being the first time Murder had ever left American soil. He was really enjoying the well-needed vacation.

Once back at the hotel suite that night, Murder had a few important phone calls that needed to be made. There was pressing business back in Philly that needed his attention. Most of all, the business he needed Quana to square away for him. He hit her up to have a conversation.

"Hello!" Quana answered.

"What up, Quana. How you?"

"I'm good, bro. Hope you enjoying your trip. You and that bougie broad of yours." Her dislike of Charlotte had no end to it.

"I am. Everything is love here. I feel like Mary J. Blige, no more drama in my life. At least not while I'm here. But then again, I don't know. That's another story for another day. The business we got to get situated with Tatiana is now top priority. That shit been heavy on my mind," he said to his sister.

Quana knew Murder way better than he thought she did. And due to her knowing how to read between the lines of his speech, she had a pretty good idea things weren't going so smoothly between he and Charlotte as he tried to make it appear to be. But she didn't bother to dig in at it, she just let it alone for another day as he said and allowed him to proceed.

Tatiana needed help in the worst way. Murder knew this. He also had knowledge that he was her only hope at getting a lawyer and to have money placed on her inmate account to hold her down throughout the ordeal. If he failed to take care of her in these two areas, he would risk her running to the police and telling all she knew. Also, putting out a hit on her life would do no good at this particular point. They would have no way to get to her. Therefore, the best thing he could do from there was to appease her in every way he knew how.

"Look, Quana, I need you to go visit Tati tomorrow, ok? Put a thousand dollars on her account for me and let her know that in the next couple of weeks, I'll have her a lawyer to help get her out of this situation. Be sure to get her to talk as much as you can about what all they may have on her, if possible. That way, I'll know what to prepare for," Murder stated.

Quana sighed in a reluctant manner, like she really didn't give a damn if Tatiana lived or died. Nonetheless, she knew how important it was to cater to the girl so she'd keep her mouth closed.

"If that's what you need me to do, bro, then know that it's done. But keep in mind, the very first opportunity we get to do what's necessary, we need to have that bitch dealt with! Like, on God, we do!" Quana spat.

"You think I don't know that? Why you think I'm now sending you and eventually Mommy too, so to keep the girl calm and not feeling abandoned or threatened.

"Ok. I was just saying. And even if that means we gotta begin our search to find a female hitter on the inside to get at the bitch, so be it. We have to take action."

"Quana! I got all that! I'm aware how much you now hate the girl behind Heeme. I know cum can be thicker than blood at times. But first things first. And that's the way I wanna do things, understood? Now I'mma call you back tomorrow night for an update. Big bro loves you and be easy."

"I love you too, bro."

The call came to an end. The two went on with what they were doing.

Chapter 23

One Day Later . . .

Quana took the task of doing what her brother had told her to do. Murder's orders came with a bit of push back, because of how much Quana despised Tatiana. But nonetheless, he was taken seriously and wasn't disrespected in the least.

Prior to the visit taking place, Quana did put the thousand bucks on Tatiana's inmate account through the payment system in place for the purpose.

Tatiana appeared in the visiting room to be greeted by an angry looking Quana. They were separated by a thick glass casing. That was probably the only thing in place to save Tatiana from being killed. Tatiana knew that if anything, Murder was the one who sent Quana to visit her, because Quana sure as hell wouldn't have done so on her own accord.

Tatiana slowly lifted the phone from the stationary hook and placed it to her ear. The two hadn't seen or heard from one another since the day of the shooting.

"Don't be sitting there looking on at me all crazy and shit, bitch!" spat Quana. "You already should know I'm only here because my brother told me to come check on you."

Tatiana looked at Quana with a downcast expression dressed over her face. Finally, she spoke up.

"Quana, thank you for coming and checking on me, whether your brother had you to do so or not. And I got the notice about the money too. Tell Barry thanks, that I love him, and that there's nothing to fear." Her words came out slowly and properly.

"There's nothing to fear, huh? I damn sure hope not. But, what all they got on you?" Quana began to inquire now. "You need to be getting busy telling me everything right now, Tatiana. And I'm talking about everything. This is for the sake of me, for the sake of you, for the sake of my brother, and for the sake of all of our freedom."

"It's nothing that'll place two of us in trouble. It's only one person who got the legal problems here. They got me charged with capital murder. All on account of a boyfriend of mine named LaShawn Norton, a UPS worker. He was the one who set me up while we were in a motel room in Cherry Hill, New Jersey. The Super 8 Motel. LaShawn was the one who booked the room in his name. Not long after we'd gotten done having sex, the cops came storming in. They had the both of us cuffed at first, but then turned him loose. That's how I knew it was a set-up. I guess he had it in mind to fuck me good and then have me locked up. For something that he did to a woman he was obsessed with. A woman who he stalked and killed. So please be sure to tell Barry my exact words, ok? He should know how to break down and get the message that's there for him. And about you and me, we should be able to bury the hatchet at a later date with the beef we got going on over Heeme, since the both of us find ourselves in love with him. And now, we gotta find a way to resolve the issue. Even if that means we all are gonna have to live together once I get this over with here. Me, you, and Heeme living under the same roof."

Tatiana stated all she felt the need to, without any level of fear. Quana didn't have any opportunity to respond. Tatiana hurried and placed the phone back on the hook, leaving a now pissed off Quana without the last word.

Quana balled up her face and squinted her eyes. She had no choice but to leave the Tatiana's actions as they were, although she'd taken them as disrespectful.

Once Tatiana got up and went back to the lock-up pod, Quana rose from her seat and exited the jail. She got into the rental car and drove away. She then began to text her brother utilizing the speech-to-text option on her phone. Everything Tatiana related was passed on to Murder.

Quana was made to think about Heeme, being that Tatiana mentioned his name. She had a phone number to a few of Heeme's people. His mother most importantly. However, no matter how bad Quana wanted to talk to him and possibly meet up to make things right, her sense of judgment warned her that it was best not to do so. To not contact anyone on Heeme's team, let alone him. There was no need to make matters any worse than they already were.

Tears appeared in Quana's eyes as she drove. Her vision was impaired and she had a hard time seeing. Anytime she thought of Heeme, her emotions would get the best of her. But at the particular time, being rational and doing the deeds her brother demanded, took rule over all else. She knew he was trying to safeguard and protect them.

Also, there was a need for Quana to find the love and respect for Tatiana once more, because at any particular moment, Tatiana could vehemently spew to the cops all she knew and have the both her and Murder locked away, to free herself of the crime.

However, Tatiana chose to stay committed to being loyal to the code and not rat on anyone. She held dear to the trust that her cousin Murder would eventually be able to locate the Norton dude and have him put down. The enterprise had to be protected. At all costs, Tatiana knew her people didn't play and would find a way to strike, then make things better. She only needed to keep quiet, remain patient, and allow the process to play itself out.

As far as Tatiana and Quana's concerns with Heeme, they had work to do. A whole lot of work to correct that situation. Quana thought long and deep over it all. Maybe a little more than she should have. He was causing more trouble than the thought was worth.

Wham!

Quana had blown threw a traffic light and ran into the driver's side door of an SUV. The disturbing part to that was, she didn't have on a seatbelt. Her body had jarred upwards onto the steering wheel, causing heavy internal injury. Possibly a loss of the unborn child she carried.

Chapter 24

Meanwhile . . .

Prior to the day of the visit between Quana and Tatiana, there was a female who was in the same day-room as Tatiana, who got in contact with a homicide detective about her through the court appointed lawyer over her case. Roberta Thompson, known on the streets as "BeeBee Thompson," was the homeless crackhead who was there the night Quana took shots at Heeme and Tatiana, and made the mistake of killing an innocent woman behind her reckless behavior.

BeeBee still had Detective Arnold Spector's contact card and needed to speak with him right away so as to try and negotiate her way out of the armed robbery and aggravated assault charges she'd racked up. She was at a junkie's haven motel, getting high with a white guy when the robbing and slashing took place.

Detective Specter appeared at the county jail to interview BeeBee, and to hear what all she may have to say. Her mind was clear and she was sober now, Specter reasoned. It may be worth his time and energy.

BeeBee was already in the interview room on the Friday afternoon Specter paid her a visit. Tatiana had been under arrest and detained for only two days. BeeBee had seen the news related to her being captured and knew who she was the moment the jail guards brought her through the door of the day-room.

"Look, lady, it's Friday. I'm ready to go home to be with my wife and daughter, and I don't have time for any bullshit. This better be worth it," Specter stated emphatically at BeeBee. Her court-appointed lawyer was there as well.

BeeBee looked on at Specter and smiled. She then turned and faced her attorney to ask a question.

"Do I have permission to speak now?" she asked.

The freshly cornrowed and sober minded inmate was granted the leeway to address the policeman. "Go ahead, Miss Thompson. Please inform Detective Specter on all you've stated to me in private," replied the female public defender.

"I do not intend to waste your time, sir. Not in the least," said BeeBee.

"God knows I hope not. But anyway, what you got for me?"

"I don't know if you remember me or not."

"—I don't," Specter shot back quickly. "So why don't you refresh my memory, if you will."

"You gave me a contact card one night."

"I've given out a million of those things in my career as an officer. You have to be more specific with me, so I'll know exactly what this relates to," Specter demanded.

"It was a shooting that occurred over in West Philly maybe a month and a half ago. An older woman caught a stray to the head as she sat in her living room watching TV. She was killed."

"A Ms. Susan Williams. Yeah, I recall that particular incident."

"I'm the witness you and another officer spoke with, and I told y'all everything I saw before, during, and after the shooting. I mentioned about the pretty little mixed girl who lived in the house across the street from the lady who got killed, that somebody in a small black shiny sports car, jumped out and started shooting at her and some guy driving another car? Does this bring back anything to mind?" BeeBee stated.

Specter pulled his phone from the belt-clip to check the notes he'd made on the case.

"Roberta Thompson?" he asked.

BeeBee spread her arms wide and raised her head in the *what's up"* position. "The one and only, live and in the flesh," she let out with a smile.

"I'm glad I mentioned you in my notes, or else, I wouldn't have had any idea who you were. You look totally different now."

"Sober and clean is what you trying to say, sir?" BeeBee smiled behind her own words.

"Well . . . yeah . . . if that's how you wish to term it. But anyway. I'm here. Talk."

"I got some news you could use, only if you're willing to drop these robbery and agg assault charges, for information that may help you solve that homicide case of the old lady," said BeeBee, the fifty-four-year-old recovering drug addict.

"Only if it's really helpful. But continue. I'm listening," responded Specter.

"That pretty little mixed girl I said who was shot at?"

"Ah-huh."

"Well, so happens, she's here in the county jail now as we speak. And the both of us are in the same day-room. She's the one who was arrested and accused of killing the mayor's niece. If you talk to her, she might be willing to give you some information about who it was that was shooting at her. Because, from the looks of things on the news, that girl needs all the help she could get!"

The interview with BeeBee continued on for an hour more. Following this, Specter contacted the lead detective over the Shavika Felton slaying, and related to him what he now knew of the accused. Together they would eventually get around to interviewing Tatiana together. But in the meantime, BeeBee's information was utilized to secure a search warrant of Tatiana's house over in West Philly. There was a lot of crucial material there that could be recovered. BeeBee was a godsend for both detectives.

Epilogue

The date was now December 21, four days away from the Christmas holiday. Charlotte and her daughter Ni'Asia were nearly done with gift wrapping presents on hand for family members flying in from Trinidad and friends who had plans to visit as well. Charlotte held plans to be the host for dinner this year.

There was a few online purchases Charlotte made that were running late on delivery. However, the dealers vowed the items would be there on her doorstep at least two days prior to Christmas, or they'd allow a return with a full refund without any problems. These were offers Charlotte couldn't help but to take on. She'd fallen back to her old way of exercising "retail therapy," a luxury she enjoyed while with Reign Man, but now, having the same leeway with Murder. Also, Charlotte appeared happier with the new sweetheart.

She and Murder did find a home in Philly to their liking and made a large deposit to secure the property. It was located in the upper Germantown section of the city in a posh and affluent neighborhood. Murder was able to convince her that the best time to make the move would be in the first or second week in January of the new year, once the holidays passed basically. But truly, this was an extension of time Murder needed to track down Heeme, so he assumed, and kill him once and for all to eliminate the threat Heeme posed. He didn't want the concerns over Charlotte and Ni'Asia's safety and well-being by placing them in harm's way while a beef was going on. Also, Charlotte was five weeks pregnant with Murder's seed. Therefore, every precautionary measure had to be taken to keep his family safe.

Murder and the hitters he had lined up alongside him, had a far more difficult time looking for Heeme than initially thought. No one had the drop on him. It was as if dude was a phantom who only existed in the mind of those who sought to get him. And whether they knew it or not, Heeme was two steps ahead of them while they remained four steps behind.

The time was just past 6:00 P.M. The sun was near full setting and darkness was upon the city.

Bong . . . Bong!

The doorbell to Charlotte's home was buzzing twice. She was under the impression that maybe it was the package delivery guy, being that she'd last checked her Amazon account and was notified that her orders would be arriving by 8:00 P.M. that day. She sent her daughter to the door to retrieve and sign for the items, because of how preoccupied she was with trying to complete the gift wrapping on the floor in the den area.

Ni'Asia did what her mother asked of her and made steps to the front door. The little girl didn't even bother to ask who was there, already thinking it was the delivery man. She opened it and was met by a smiling man in a dark brown colored pair of khakis and button-up shirt.

"You the package delivery man, right?" she asked from pure innocence.

The man at their front door also had on an elegant Christmas themed sweater over the Dickie top he had on and maintained a friendly smile. There was a beautifully wrapped gift box in his hands to go along with the welcoming energy he gave off.

"Hey there! How you doing? And yes, I am the delivery man. I got a package for the lovely lady of the house. Would that be you, or your mom?" the clean-cut, pleasant-faced man asked.

"More than likely, that would be my mom. She told me to sign for it," Ni'Asia answered.

"It's something from a guy named Barry. Do you know who he is?"

The youngster smiled in delight at the question, also at the thought of how happy her mother was going to be once she knew of another gift her boyfriend had bought for her. Ni'Asia knew all about the ring, the necklace, and her sibling that was on the way. She became ecstatic.

"Yeah, I know who Barry is. He's my mom's boyfriend," she answered.

"Is it just you and your mom or is anyone else here with you two?" the man asked.

"It's just me and my mom, like it is most days," Ni'Asia responded, still smiling gracefully.

"Bring your ass here, you little bitch!" the man hissed in a menacing tone of voice as he aggressively grabbed hold of Ni'Asia. He began to choke her with his left arm and covered her mouth with the right hand upon barging into the house.

Charlotte had the volume to the music a little louder than she normally would. This prevented her from hearing the light thud of the man's gift box hitting the floor, along with her ceramic vase that was knocked over by the door.

With the little girl yoked tightly in the throes of his arms, the intruder speedily walked through the house in the direction from where the music came from.

The door to the den where Charlotte was situated was opened. She bobbed her head and grooved to the beat playing. The man appeared in the doorway of the room with Ni'Asia in one arm and an automatic pistol in the hand of the other, now trained on Charlotte.

Upon raising her head and taking notice of what was unfolding, Charlotte immediately responded with submission. Her mouth flew open and she burst into tears. She whimpered and sobbed.

"Please! No! I'll give you whatever you want. Just don't do anything to me and my daughter. Please! I'm begging you!" Charlotte's words struggled to come out. They'd gotten hung up in her throat.

The intruder turned into a madman. He aggressively shoved the frail little Ni'Asia from his clutches down towards her mother, causing her to sprain her arm upon making contact with the floor. He then rushed over and maliciously kicked Charlotte in the face. She was nearly knocked out behind the assault. Dude yanked Ni'Asia's sneakers off for the laces, then proceeded to tie the mother and daughter together tightly.

Charlotte spit a thick glob of blood from her mouth onto the carpet. She was badly disoriented and possibly suffered a concussion.

"What is it you want?" she moaned to slur out.

"Bitch! Where the fuck you keeping the cash and the kilos of dope you holding for that nigga Murder?" Heeme spat. "I know it's in here somewhere," he continued, gritting his teeth. He reached down and grabbed her phone from the floor. "What's the pass code to unlock this motherfucka', bitch!"

Her phone had a pattern lock code to it.

Charlotte and her daughter both began to cry endlessly it seemed.

"The pattern is a capital letter 'N,' start at the bottom left corner and go up," she explained but struggled to do so.

Heeme drew out the pattern to unlock the device. "There. Got it! Now, what number in the contacts or name do I go to that belongs to the nigga Murder!" he further demanded.

"Who is this Murder that you're talking about?"

Heeme looked down at her with a face of disgust. "What!"

Wham!

He kicked her once more in the face.

172

"Bitch, stop playing with me! Don't act like you don't know that Murder and Barry are the same person. Because that shit will get you and that little whore there whacked quickly!"

"Barry. It's under the name Barry," Charlotte confessed.

Heeme hit the phone icon to call Murder and awaited him to answer.

"Yeah, what's up, baby? How is everything going with the gift wrapping?" he answered upon notice of the number.

Heeme had the phone on speaker.

"Everything going fine with the gifts, nigga! Thanks in advance!" spat Heeme in reply.

"What the fuck? Who dis?" Murder asked in a shocked tone. He managed to match aggressiveness.

"It's the nigga who you love to hate, and the nigga who you hated your sister to love! Catch me if you can, pussy-boy! Because once I take all your money and bricks of dope I'm sure you got stashed here, I'mma kill you, nigga! And if I walk away empty-handed, I'mma kill these two who I already got tied up here, before I get to you!"

Murder finally caught onto the voice.

"Heeme! What the fuck, nigga!? How the hell you know where my lady live!?"

"That's besides the point, nigga! It don't matter how I know. But what does matter is that you better hand me back my motherfuckin' money, and my bricks of heroin that stank-ass sister of yours stole from me. And as an addition, I'mma gon ahead and wipe your nose now, for everything that I find here in this house. It's gonna be *bang-bang, bye-bye,* for these two bitches here with no questions asked and no more negotiations! Now, where my shit?" Heeme spat then killed the call and turned off the phone.

His intentions from there was to kidnap Charlotte and Ni'Asia and transport them back to Philly in the trunk until Murder paid the ransom.

"Sir, please! Me and my daughter don't have anything to do with what you and Barry got going on. Okay, si —"

"Shut the fuck up, bitch! I ain't ask you to say shit!" he stated, cutting her words short.

"Sir, please, I'm pregnant." Charlotte continued to plead for mercy.

"You think I give a motherfuck about you being pregnant? Huh! I couldn't care less! So miss me with the bullshit!" He leaned over and barked directly in Charlotte's face.

Heeme raised up tall again and turned towards the direction of the room door. He was intent on going to the living room once more to have a look out the front door to be sure no one was coming there for Charlotte. On a random visit or otherwise. He also thought he'd heard someone attempting to enter.

Suddenly, he stopped in his tracks and turned to face Charlotte once more to bark further. He was now really pissed at the thought of Murder and Quana and was at a boiling point to kill them both. And in a vicious type of way.

"Bitch, you better —"

BANG!

A gunshot rang out, cutting his words short. It was a head shot upon someone. They never saw it coming.

To Be Continued . . .

COMING SOON

THESE VICIOUS STREETS 4
In For A Penny In For A Pound

THESE VICIOUS STREETS 5
No Love No Glory

Lock Down Publications and Ca$h Presents
Assisted Publishing Packages

BASIC PACKAGE	UPGRADED PACKAGE
$499	$800
Editing	Typing
Cover Design	Editing
Formatting	Cover Design
	Formatting
ADVANCE PACKAGE	**LDP SUPREME PACKAGE**
$1,200	$1,500
Typing	Typing
Editing	Editing
Cover Design	Cover Design
Formatting	Formatting
Copyright registration	Copyright registration
Proofreading	Proofreading
Upload book to Amazon	Set up Amazon account
	Upload book to Amazon
	Advertise on LDP, Amazon and
	Facebook Page

***Other services available upon request.
Additional charges may apply

Lock Down Publications
P.O. Box 944
Stockbridge, GA 30281-9998
Phone: 470 303-9761

Submission Guideline

Submit the first three chapters of your completed manuscript to ldpsubmissions@gmail.com. In the subject line add **Your Book's Title**. The manuscript must be in a Word Doc file and sent as an attachment. Document should be in Times New Roman, double spaced, and in size 12 font. Also, provide your synopsis and full contact information. If sending multiple submissions, they must each be in a separate email.

Have a story but no way to send it electronically? You can still submit to LDP/Ca$h Presents. Send in the first three chapters, written or typed, of your completed manuscript to:

LDP: Submissions Dept
P.O. Box 944
Stockbridge, GA 30281-9998

DO NOT send original manuscript. Must be a duplicate. Provide your synopsis and a cover letter containing your full contact information.

Thanks for considering LDP and Ca$h Presents.

NEW RELEASES

BLOODLINE OF A SAVAGE 1&2
THESE VICIOUS STREETS 1&2
RELENTLESS GOON
RELENTLESS GOON 2
BY PRINCE A. TAUHID

THE BUTTERFLY MAFIA 1-3
BY FUMIYA PAYNE

A THUG'S STREET PRINCESS 1&2
BY MEESHA

CITY OF SMOKE 2
BY MOLOTTI

STEPPERS 1,2&3
THE REAL BADDIES OF CHI-RAQ
BY KING RIO

THE LANE 1&2
BY KEN-KEN SPENCE

THUG OF SPADES 1&2
LOVE IN THE TRENCHES 2
CORNER BOYS
BY COREY ROBINSON

TIL DEATH 3
BY ARYANNA

THE BIRTH OF A GANGSTER 4
BY DELMONT PLAYER

PRODUCT OF THE STREETS 1&2
BY DEMOND "MONEY" ANDERSON

NO TIME FOR ERROR
BY KEESE

MONEY HUNGRY DEMONS
BY TRANAY ADAMS

Coming Soon from Lock Down Publications/Ca$h Presents

IF YOU CROSS ME ONCE 6
ANGEL V
By Anthony Fields

IMMA DIE BOUT MINE 5
By Aryanna

A THUGS STREET PRINCESS 3
By Meesha

PRODUCT OF THE STREETS 3
By Demond Money Anderson

CORNER BOYS 2
By Corey Robinson

THE MURDER QUEENS 6&7
By Michael Gallon

CITY OF SMOKE 3
By Molotti

CONFESSIONS OF A DOPE BOY
By Nicholas Lock

THA TAKEOVER
By Keith Chandler

BETRAYAL OF A G 2
By Ray Vinci

CRIME BOSS
By Playa Ray

Available Now

RESTRAINING ORDER 1 & 2
By **CA$H & Coffee**

LOVE KNOWS NO BOUNDARIES 1-3
By **Coffee**

RAISED AS A GOON I, II, III & IV
BRED BY THE SLUMS I, II, III
BLAST FOR ME I & II
ROTTEN TO THE CORE I II III
A BRONX TALE I, II, III
DUFFLE BAG CARTEL I II III IV V VI
HEARTLESS GOON I II III IV V
A SAVAGE DOPEBOY I II
DRUG LORDS I II III
CUTTHROAT MAFIA I II
KING OF THE TRENCHES
By **Ghost**

LAY IT DOWN I & II
LAST OF A DYING BREED I II
BLOOD STAINS OF A SHOTTA I & II III
By **Jamaica**

LOYAL TO THE GAME I II III
LIFE OF SIN I, II III
By **TJ & Jelissa**

IF LOVING HIM IS WRONG…I & II
LOVE ME EVEN WHEN IT HURTS I II III
By **Jelissa**

PUSH IT TO THE LIMIT
By **Bre' Hayes**

BLOODY COMMAS I & II
SKI MASK CARTEL I, II & III
KING OF NEW YORK I II, III IV V
RISE TO POWER I II III
COKE KINGS I II III IV V
BORN HEARTLESS I II III IV
KING OF THE TRAP I II
By **T.J. Edwards**

WHEN THE STREETS CLAP BACK I & II III
THE HEART OF A SAVAGE I II III IV
MONEY MAFIA I II
LOYAL TO THE SOIL I II III
By **Jibril Williams**

A DISTINGUISHED THUG STOLE MY HEART I II & III
LOVE SHOULDN'T HURT I II III IV
RENEGADE BOYS 1-4
PAID IN KARMA 1-3
SAVAGE STORMS 1-3
AN UNFORESEEN LOVE 1-3
BABY, I'M WINTERTIME COLD 1-3
A THUG'S STREET PRINCESS 1&2
By **Meesha**

A GANGSTER'S CODE 1-3
A GANGSTER'S SYN 1-3
THE SAVAGE LIFE 1-3
CHAINED TO THE STREETS 1-3
BLOOD ON THE MONEY 1-3
A GANGSTA'S PAIN 1-3
BEAUTIFUL LIES AND UGLY TRUTHS
CHURCH IN THESE STREETS
By **J-Blunt**

CUM FOR ME 1-8
An LDP Erotica Collaboration

BLOOD OF A BOSS 1-5
SHADOWS OF THE GAME
TRAP BASTARD
By **Askari**

THE STREETS BLEED MURDER 1-3
THE HEART OF A GANGSTA 1-3
By **Jerry Jackson**

WHEN A GOOD GIRL GOES BAD
By **Adrienne**

THE COST OF LOYALTY 1-3
By **Kweli**

BRIDE OF A HUSTLA 1-3
THE FETTI GIRLS 1-3
CORRUPTED BY A GANGSTA 1-4
BLINDED BY HIS LOVE
THE PRICE YOU PAY FOR LOVE 1-3
DOPE GIRL MAGIC 1-3
By **Destiny Skai**

A KINGPIN'S AMBITION
A KINGPIN'S AMBITION II
I MURDER FOR THE DOUGH
By **Ambitious**

TRUE SAVAGE 1-7
DOPE BOY MAGIC 1-3
MIDNIGHT CARTEL 1-3
CITY OF KINGZ 1&2
NIGHTMARE ON SILENT AVE
THE PLUG OF LIL MEXICO 1&2
CLASSIC CITY
By **Chris Green**

A GANGSTER'S REVENGE 1-4
THE BOSS MAN'S DAUGHTERS 1-5
A SAVAGE LOVE 1&2
BAE BELONGS TO ME 1&2
A HUSTLER'S DECEIT 1-3
WHAT BAD BITCHES DO 1-3
SOUL OF A MONSTER 1-3
KILL ZONE
A DOPE BOY'S QUEEN 1-3
TIL DEATH 1-3
IMMA DIE BOUT MINE 1-4
By **Aryanna**

A DOPEBOY'S PRAYER
By **Eddie "Wolf" Lee**

THE KING CARTEL 1-3
By **Frank Gresham**

THESE NIGGAS AIN'T LOYAL 1-3
By **Nikki Tee**

GANGSTA SHYT 1-3
By **CATO**

THE ULTIMATE BETRAYAL
By **Phoenix**

BOSS'N UP 1-3
By **Royal Nicole**

I LOVE YOU TO DEATH
By **Destiny J**

I RIDE FOR MY HITTA
I STILL RIDE FOR MY HITTA
By **Misty Holt**

LOVE & CHASIN' PAPER
By **Qay Crockett**

TO DIE IN VAIN
SINS OF A HUSTLA
By **ASAD**

BROOKLYN HUSTLAZ
By **Boogsy Morina**

BROOKLYN ON LOCK 1 & 2
By **Sonovia**

GANGSTA CITY
By **Teddy Duke**

A DRUG KING AND HIS DIAMOND 1-3
A DOPEMAN'S RICHES
HER MAN, MINE'S TOO 1&2
CASH MONEY HO'S
THE WIFEY I USED TO BE 1&2
PRETTY GIRLS DO NASTY THINGS
By **Nicole Goosby**

LIPSTICK KILLAH 1-3
CRIME OF PASSION 1-3
FRIEND OR FOE 1-3
By **Mimi**

TRAPHOUSE KING 1-3
KINGPIN KILLAZ 1-3
STREET KINGS 1&2
PAID IN BLOOD 1&2
CARTEL KILLAZ 1-3
DOPE GODS 1&2
By **Hood Rich**

THE STREETS ARE CALLING
By **Duquie Wilson**

STEADY MOBBN' 1-3
THE STREETS STAINED MY SOUL 1-3
By **Marcellus Allen**

WHO SHOT YA 1-3
SON OF A DOPE FIEND 1-4
HEAVEN GOT A GHETTO 1&2
SKI MASK MONEY 1&2
By **Renta**

GORILLAZ IN THE BAY 1-4
TEARS OF A GANGSTA 1/&2
3X KRAZY 1&2
STRAIGHT BEAST MODE 1&2
By **DE'KARI**

TRIGGADALE 1-3
MURDA WAS THE CASE 1-3
By **Elijah R. Freeman**

SLAUGHTER GANG 1-3
RUTHLESS HEART 1-3
By **Willie Slaughter**

GOD BLESS THE TRAPPERS 1-3
THESE SCANDALOUS STREETS 1-3
FEAR MY GANGSTA 1-5
THESE STREETS DON'T LOVE NOBODY 1-2
BURY ME A G 1-5
A GANGSTA'S EMPIRE 1-4
THE DOPEMAN'S BODYGAURD 1&2
THE REALEST KILLAZ 1-3
THE LAST OF THE OGS 1-3
By **Tranay Adams**

MARRIED TO A BOSS 1-3
By **Destiny Skai & Chris Green**

KINGZ OF THE GAME 1-7
CRIME BOSS 1-3
By **Playa Ray**

FUK SHYT
By **Blakk Diamond**

DON'T F#CK WITH MY HEART 1&2
By **Linnea**

ADDICTED TO THE DRAMA 1-3
IN THE ARM OF HIS BOSS
By **Jamila**

LOYALTY AIN'T PROMISED 1&2
By **Keith Williams**

YAYO 1-4
A SHOOTER'S AMBITION 1&2
BRED IN THE GAME
By **S. Allen**

TRAP GOD 1-3
RICH $AVAGE 1-3
MONEY IN THE GRAVE 1-3
CARTEL MONEY
By **Martell Troublesome Bolden**

FOREVER GANGSTA 1&2
GLOCKS ON SATIN SHEETS 1&2
By **Adrian Dulan**

TOE TAGZ 1-4
LEVELS TO THIS SHYT 1&2
IT'S JUST ME AND YOU
By **Ah'Million**

KINGPIN DREAMS 1-3
RAN OFF ON DA PLUG
By **Paper Boi Rari**

THE STREETS MADE ME 1-3
By **Larry D. Wright**

CONFESSIONS OF A GANGSTA 1-4
CONFESSIONS OF A JACKBOY 1-3
CONFESSIONS OF A HITMAN
By **Nicholas Lock**

I'M NOTHING WITHOUT HIS LOVE
SINS OF A THUG
TO THE THUG I LOVED BEFORE
A GANGSTA SAVED XMAS
IN A HUSTLER I TRUST
By **Monet Dragun**

QUIET MONEY 1-3
THUG LIFE 1-3
EXTENDED CLIP 1&2
A GANGSTA'S PARADISE
By **Trai'Quan**

CAUGHT UP IN THE LIFE 1-3
THE STREETS NEVER LET GO 1-3
By **Robert Baptiste**

NEW TO THE GAME 1-3
MONEY, MURDER & MEMORIES 1-3
By **Malik D. Rice**

CREAM 2-3
THE STREETS WILL TALK
By **Yolanda Moore**

THE STREETS WILL NEVER CLOSE 1-3
By **K'ajji**

LIFE OF A SAVAGE 1-4
A GANGSTA'S QUR'AN 1-4
MURDA SEASON 1-3
GANGLAND CARTEL 1-3
CHI'RAQ GANGSTAS 1-4
KILLERS ON ELM STREET 1-3
JACK BOYZ N DA BRONX 1-3
A DOPEBOY'S DREAM 1-3
JACK BOYS VS DOPE BOYS 1-3
COKE GIRLZ
COKE BOYS
SOSA GANG 1&2
BRONX SAVAGES
BODYMORE KINGPINS
BLOOD OF A GOON
By **Romell Tukes**

CONCRETE KILLA 1-3
VICIOUS LOYALTY 1-3
By **Kingpen**

THE ULTIMATE SACRIFICE 1-6
KHADIFI
IF YOU CROSS ME ONCE 1-3
ANGEL 1-4
IN THE BLINK OF AN EYE
By **Anthony Fields**

THE LIFE OF A HOOD STAR
By **Ca$h & Rashia Wilson**

NIGHTMARES OF A HUSTLA 1-3
BLOOD AND GAMES 1&2
By **King Dream**

GHOST MOB
By **Stilloan Robinson**

HARD AND RUTHLESS 1&2
MOB TOWN 251
THE BILLIONAIRE BENTLEYS 1-3
REAL G'S MOVE IN SILENCE
By **Von Diesel**

MOB TIES 1-7
SOUL OF A HUSTLER, HEART OF A KILLER 1-3
GORILLAZ IN THE TRENCHES
By **SayNoMore**

BODYMORE MURDERLAND 1-3
THE BIRTH OF A GANGSTER 1-4
By **Delmont Player**

FOR THE LOVE OF A BOSS 1&2
By **C. D. Blue**

KILLA KOUNTY 1-5
By **Khufu**

MOBBED UP 1-4
THE BRICK MAN 1-5
THE COCAINE PRINCESS 1-10
STEPPERS 1-3
SUPER GREMLIN 1-4
By **King Rio**

MONEY GAME 1&2
By **Smoove Dolla**

A GANGSTA'S KARMA 1-4
By **FLAME**

KING OF THE TRENCHES 1-3
By **GHOST & TRANAY ADAMS**

QUEEN OF THE ZOO 1&2
By **Black Migo**

GRIMEY WAYS 1-3
BETRAYAL OF A G
By **Ray Vinci**

XMAS WITH AN ATL SHOOTER
By **Ca$h & Destiny Skai**

KING KILLA 1&2
By **Vincent "Vitto" Holloway**

BETRAYAL OF A THUG 1&2
By **Fre$h**

THE MURDER QUEENS 1-5
By **Michael Gallon**

FOR THE LOVE OF BLOOD 1-4
By **Jamel Mitchell**

HOOD CONSIGLIERE 1&2
NO TIME FOR ERROR
By **Keese**

PROTÉGÉ OF A LEGEND 1&2
LOVE IN THE TRENCHES 1&2
By **Corey Robinson**

THE PLUG'S RUTHLESS DAUGHTER
By **Tony Daniels**

BORN IN THE GRAVE 1-3
CRIME PAYS
By **Self Made Tay**

MOAN IN MY MOUTH
By **XTASY**

TORN BETWEEN A GANGSTER AND A GENTLEMAN
By **J-BLUNT & Miss Kim**

LOYALTY IS EVERYTHING 1-3
CITY OF SMOKE 1&2
By **Molotti**

HERE TODAY GONE TOMORROW 1&2
By **Fly Rock**

WOMEN LIE MEN LIE 1-4
FIFTY SHADES OF SNOW 1-3
STACK BEFORE YOU SPLURGE
GIRLS FALL LIKE DOMINOES
NAÏVE TO THE STREETS
By **ROY MILLIGAN**

PILLOW PRINCESS
By **S. Hawkins**

THE BUTTERFLY MAFIA 1-3
SALUTE MY SAVAGERY 1&2
By **Fumiya Payne**

THE LANE 1&2
By Ken-Ken Spence

THE PUSSY TRAP 1-5
By **Nene Capri**

DIRTY DNA
By **Blaque**

SANCTIFIED AND HORNY
by **XTASY**

BOOKS BY LDP'S CEO, CA$H

TRUST IN NO MAN
TRUST IN NO MAN 2
TRUST IN NO MAN 3
BONDED BY BLOOD
SHORTY GOT A THUG
THUGS CRY
THUGS CRY 2
THUGS CRY 3
TRUST NO BITCH
TRUST NO BITCH 2
TRUST NO BITCH 3
TIL MY CASKET DROPS
RESTRAINING ORDER
RESTRAINING ORDER 2
IN LOVE WITH A CONVICT
LIFE OF A HOOD STAR
XMAS WITH AN ATL SHOOTER

www.ingramcontent.com/pod-product-compliance
Lightning Source LLC
Chambersburg PA
CBHW070514260626
47161CB00004B/1551